BACKWOODS

BACKWOODS

Natty Soltesz

Illustrated by Michael Kirwan

QUEER MOJO
A Rebel Satori Imprint
Bar Harbor, Maine

REBEL SATORI PRESS
P.O. Box 363, Hulls Cove, ME 04644
www.rebelsatori.com

Stories have previously appeared in these books: "Mr Weist When He's At Home," *Hot Jocks* (Cleis Press); "The Opera House," *Best Gay Erotica 2009* (Cleis Press); "The Falls," *Best Gay Romance 2010* (Cleis Press); "Paperboys," *Boy Crazy* (Cleis Press); "Fuck Stuff," *Pornopticon* (Cyberpunk Apocalypse); "The Hippie Down-Low," *Best Gay Erotica 2010* (Cleis Press); "Adult," *Best Gay Romance 2009* (Cleis Press).

Thanks to Andrew Aiello-Hauser, Shane Allison, Daniel Bauer, James Champagne, Dennis Cooper, Jerome Crooks, Dario, Natty Fan, Mack Friedman, Matt Gallaway, Martin Gómez H, Headmaster Magazine, Venus "Balls" Highland, Katie Johnston, Laurie K, Richard Labonté, Sara Luby, Johnny Murdoc, Amanda O'Dell, Ryan Patterson, Jason Quest, Mike Riley, Sagas/MC Head, Yves Sauriol, Yancey Strickler, Swisschris, R Wheatley and Rob Wolfsham.

Book design by Sven Davisson
Cover & Illustrations by Michael Kirwan

ISBN: 978-1-60864-036-2

Contents

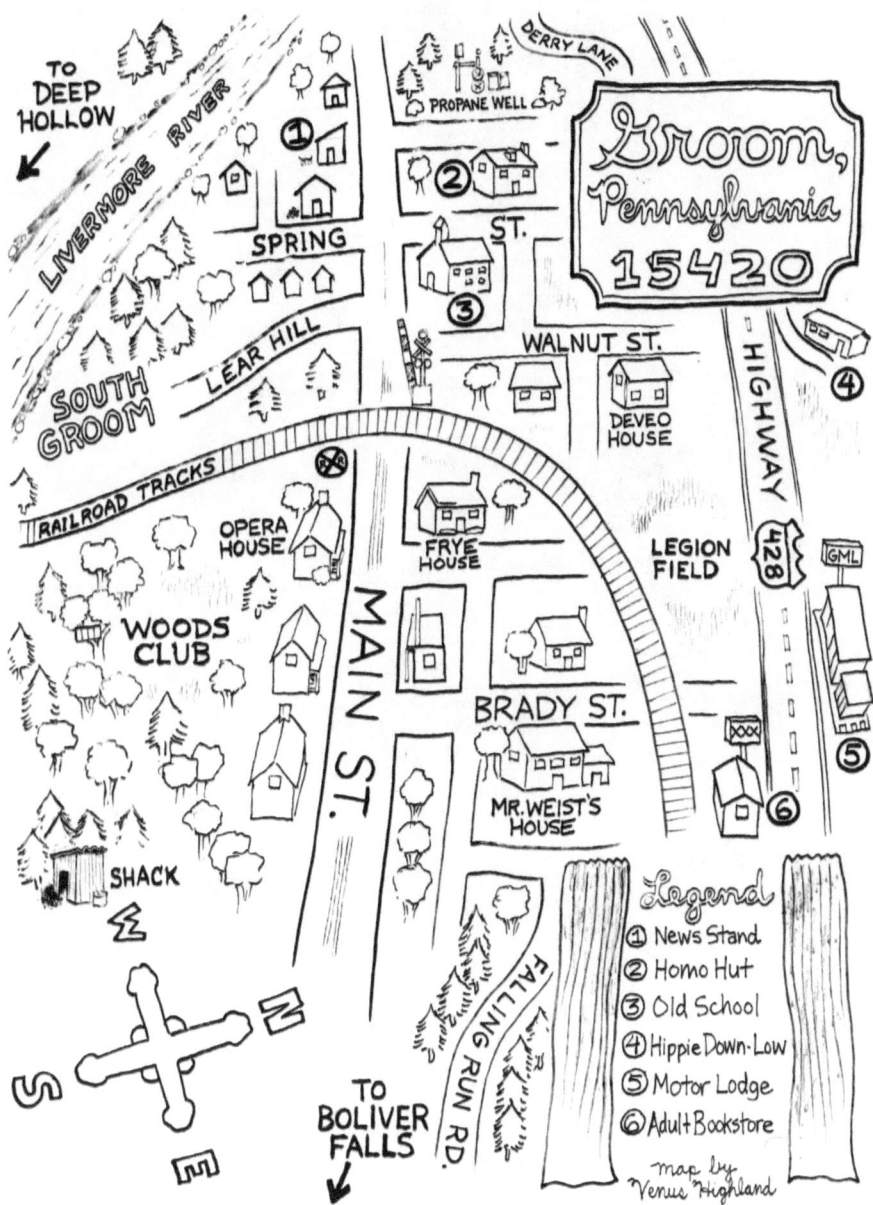

1. The Train

I'm the engineer, the guy who drives the train at night. I sit in the front of the engine car, in the cabin that's lit up inside, and I take the train where it goes.

My regular route runs from Pittsburgh to Deep Hollow and through lots of little towns in between. No stops. It's good work, slow and steady once you get over the fear of it, the responsibility of driving this huge, crashing thing.

I used to drive trucks. I didn't like that so much. Driving on the highway, you pass everything by. You can't really see a town from the highway unless you get off of it and take an inroad, and who does that? You'd get lost, and there's no point.

There's things on the highway—diners, gas stations, Wal-Marts. And if there isn't that there's those concrete walls that run for miles. They're all fronts anyway—things that keep you from seeing what's really there.

The train tracks, though, they've been there forever. They're part of the landscape. Most of these towns are built from them, not the other way around. So the train runs behind things—past backyards and back doors and on through the woods; a town's hidden places and secret spots.

I like to wonder about the places I pass through, sleepy little rural towns, towns that time forgot. The kind of places where, when the fire siren goes off, moms call their kids across town to make sure they're okay. Places with teenagers who have nothing better to do but get high in old playgrounds. Old folks, young folks, all with lives as full as anyone's.

Then sometimes I see things from the train—lit-up windows late at night. People standing on dark, empty roads, watching me.

Most times I'm alone. I don't mind that so much. You get to

feeling safe in all those back areas, feeling like nobody can see you, so you can do whatever you want.

My wife left me five years ago. I don't got any kids. I don't got any inclination to make apologies for myself or to keep myself from doing what I want, when I want.

So yeah, I jack off, just like I've jacked off at every job I've worked since I was thirteen. If I'm feeling really freaky I work it during the whole route. Take off my pants, stroke it slow till I can't stand it anymore.

There are things you can do with yourself, you know, things you sort of forget about when you get older. When you're a teenager you're so horny for yourself; you're tearing off your own clothes at every opportunity, like you're in lust for your own dick, doing every kinky or pornographic thing that comes into your head.

Least that's how I was.

After awhile, being alone on this job, I started getting that back. One night I was so horny I decided to try eating my own jizz. I shoot pretty far, anyway, so I just hauled up and aimed toward my mouth and slurped it down. Fun stuff. Didn't taste like nothing but made me horny as hell.

Then one night I started thinking about how my ex-wife used to let me stick it in her ass from time to time, and I got to wondering what it might feel like to stick a finger up my own ass. You know, nothing's keeping me from trying this stuff. So I got my index finger spit-wet and slid it up there. Shot a load damn near farther than any since I'd been pulling my pud in the junior high bathroom stall. Shot it a couple feet over my shoulder; swear to God.

Sometimes when I cum I blow the whistle, just to amuse myself. Blowing the whistle used to make me nervous—you know, just how loud it is in the night. But I think people are used to it, they just sleep right through. Still, I wonder sometimes. I wonder if the sound of it drifts into their open bedroom windows, gets into their dreams.

2. The Homo Hut

Randy Perletti woke in the dead of night. The gory red numbers on the bedside clock said 3 a.m. He felt afraid, and his sleep-addled brain scanned for the cause. It got it when he again heard the creak of his front porch floorboards. Then another sound: *clacka clacka clacka.*

He was alone. Dominic Posvar, his long-time partner, was thirty miles away at the private campground they co-owned. It was summer and Randy had left the windows open, and the door unlocked for that matter. That was something you could do in a town like Groom, Pennsylvania. Usually.

He threw off the covers and slipped on his sandals. He heard it again: *clacka clacka clacka.* Then: *hisssss.*

A spray-paint can, he realized. And just as suddenly he pieced together the likely scenario.

Randy and Dom had lived in their house on Spring Street for the past twenty-five years and in that time they'd experienced their share of harassment. It came with the territory in a rural town like Groom. Their house was inordinately pelted with hard corn, eggs, and tomatoes come October. The really nasty stuff was rarer.

Once while waiting in line at the Dairy Queen they noticed a gaggle of teenagers keep glancing at them and whispering. Randy managed to eavesdrop on their conversation.

"Those are the faggots," said a boy with zits on his lip.

"Don't call them that," said a girl.

"Who?" said another boy.

"The faggots. They live in the Homo Hut on Spring Street."

The Homo Hut. Randy was tickled, and he championed the term almost to the point of committing it to needlepoint and hanging it on their front door, an idea that Dom had mercifully

3

nixed.

Randy crept into the living room. He heard the hiss again, the creak. A shadow passed over his front window. He knelt on the couch and peeked behind the curtain. From a streetlight he could make out the silhouette of a young man wearing a baseball cap.

He had to act quickly. He stepped to the front door, grasped the knob, and counted to three. Then he whipped it open and threw forward the screen door. It hit the kid in the shoulder. Randy reached out and grabbed the first thing he felt—the kid's jacket. The kid pulled like a dog on a chain but Randy managed to grab his arm, then his neck. He dug his fingertips into the kid's neck whereupon the kid gasped and dropped his spray-paint can.

Randy yanked him through the doorway and into the hall. Blocking the front door, he switched on the hall light. He flicked off the kid's cap. He stared at Randy with wild, snarling eyes.

"Oh, you're familiar. Frye, right? Tom Frye's son?" The kid said nothing. "Dan, isn't it?"

"Lemme go," he said, but made no move toward Randy.

"I don't think so, you little shit. What'd you write out there anyway?" Randy opened the door and peeked around. On the white siding between his porch windows, in blue spray paint, was an uncompleted thought: FUCK FAGO.

"You spelled it wrong," Randy said, shutting the door again. He turned and faced young Dan just in time to catch his wandering eyes. Randy hadn't thought of the fact that he'd worn just a pair of skimpy blue briefs to bed. And, half a century old or not, Randy was no slouch. He worked hard at the campground, chopping firewood, clearing trails. He had a natural build, muscled and tan. And a big cock. Which this homophobic kid had apparently noticed.

Randy couldn't help but check out the kid himself. He had "asshole" written all over his face, but beyond that he was a piece of muscled teenage ass, with biceps bulging out the sleeves of his T-shirt, a broad chest and a tiny waist.

4

"How old are you?" Randy said.

"Eighteen," Dan said through clenched teeth. His breathing was starting to slow. Randy, thinking of how to handle it, propped his hand on his hip. The kid looked again at Randy's crotch, but when he looked up this time he knew he'd been caught. Shame flooded his face.

This wasn't some teenage prank, Randy realized. There was a reason this person was here. There was *always* a reason.

✖

Men showed up at Dom and Randy's door—usually the back door—with reasons. Excuses.

"I was wondering if I could borrow your nail gun?"

"My daughter's sick, so I'm stuck delivering the cookies."

"We had some extra maple saplings at the nursery so I thought you might want me to plant one in your yard?" That was one of Randy's favorites, from a recent regular named Alan Reynolds.

"Absolutely," Randy said. Randy had had his eye on Alan ever since he'd run into him with his family at the BiLo a few weeks prior. Alan's wife, Carol, was a local girl whose parents Randy knew well. She introduced Randy to her husband as "one of the guys who lives down on Spring Street," and from Alan's slightly alarmed but tolerant reaction, Randy could tell he was aware of his status as one-half of the town's out homo population.

"It's nice to meet you," Alan had said, lifting himself up from his slumped position over the shopping buggy. Something about the man instantly struck Randy, and it wasn't just his handsome features or toned body. It was the way he looked at the floor while his wife extolled the virtues of her remodeled kitchen. It was his faded polo shirt, and the weary way he pulled his daughters back from grabbing at things on the shelves. It was the look on his face: the look of defeat.

A week later Randy ran into Alan again when he was taking a walk. Alan was mowing the lawn in front of his house. He spotted Randy and waved to him, turning off the mower.

"Lazy Sunday, eh?" Randy said as Alan approached him.

"Yep. After I'm done here I'll probably have a go at my project in the garage," Alan said.

"Oh yeah?"

"Yeah. I've got a Fat Boy in there I'm rebuilding."

"No shit," Randy said.

"Yeah," Alan said, lifting up his faded Scorpions concert T-shirt to mop the sweat off of his face. Randy considered the T-shirt, which he figured Alan only wore when he was mowing the lawn. He considered Alan's project in the garage. Both were relics, he realized, souvenirs of Alan's life before he'd had to pack it away to make room for a family.

"I've got a Harley," Randy told him. "I take it out whenever I can." Alan's eyes lit up.

"That's fantastic," he said.

"You should stop by some time and check it out."

So Alan had come around a week or so later, maple sapling in hand. Randy had him plant it at the edge of their yard, next to the alley, and sat back to watch Alan's tall, strong frame crack the ground and turn it out. Afterwards Randy got them both a beer and led Alan to the garage.

"How's the family?" Randy asked when Alan had finished admiring Randy's Harley.

"Carol's great," Alan said, resting his butt against Randy's work table. "Kids are great. Everything's fine. You know—even-keeled," he said, making a motion with his hand as if he were sanding the rough edges from a board.

"Carol ever ride with you?" Randy asked.

"No. Not since college, anyway."

"Yeah, I try to get Dom on mine. He thinks they're too dangerous. And they are, I guess. But what's life for if not to take risks?" Alan laughed. It seemed to bubble up from some contained part of him. "Riding's just something you get an itch for, you know?"

"Absolutely," Alan agreed.

"In fact I almost got a Harley logo tattooed on me back in the day," Randy said. "Was gonna get it on my back," he said, turning and lifting his shirt to show Alan a faded flaming skull tattoo on his broad, tan back. "Got that instead."

"Nice," Alan said, a catch to his voice.

"You have any?"

"Uh, just a couple I got in college," Alan said. "One on my back." He lifted his shirt, fully aware, Randy thought, of what he was doing. There was a tribal design on his tight lower midsection, just above the waist band of his Jockeys.

"Nice. I like those," Randy said. Alan turned and pulled down his shirt. He opened his mouth as if to say something then stopped.

"You have any others?" Randy asked.

"Yeah, it's...well..." He shot Randy a quick but intense glance, then lowered the waist band of his jeans. His pelvis still had that cut, v-shape. He'd caught the band of his Jockeys in his thumb, too, and lowered them until Randy could see the little four-leaf clover that sat to the top-right of his light brown pubic patch.

"Cool," Randy said.

"I don't know what my wife would think if she knew I was showing this off," Alan said.

Randy couldn't help himself. "I won't tell her," he said, reaching out and tracing the clover with his finger. Alan quivered at the touch but didn't pull away.

"Is that a promise?" Alan said.

"Absolutely."

"What about your, uh, boyfriend?"

"Dom and I have an understanding," Randy said. There was a shape emerging against the front of Alan's jeans like a snake under the cloth. Randy grabbed hold of it and silently praised the lord. The guy was hung like a frickin donkey.

7

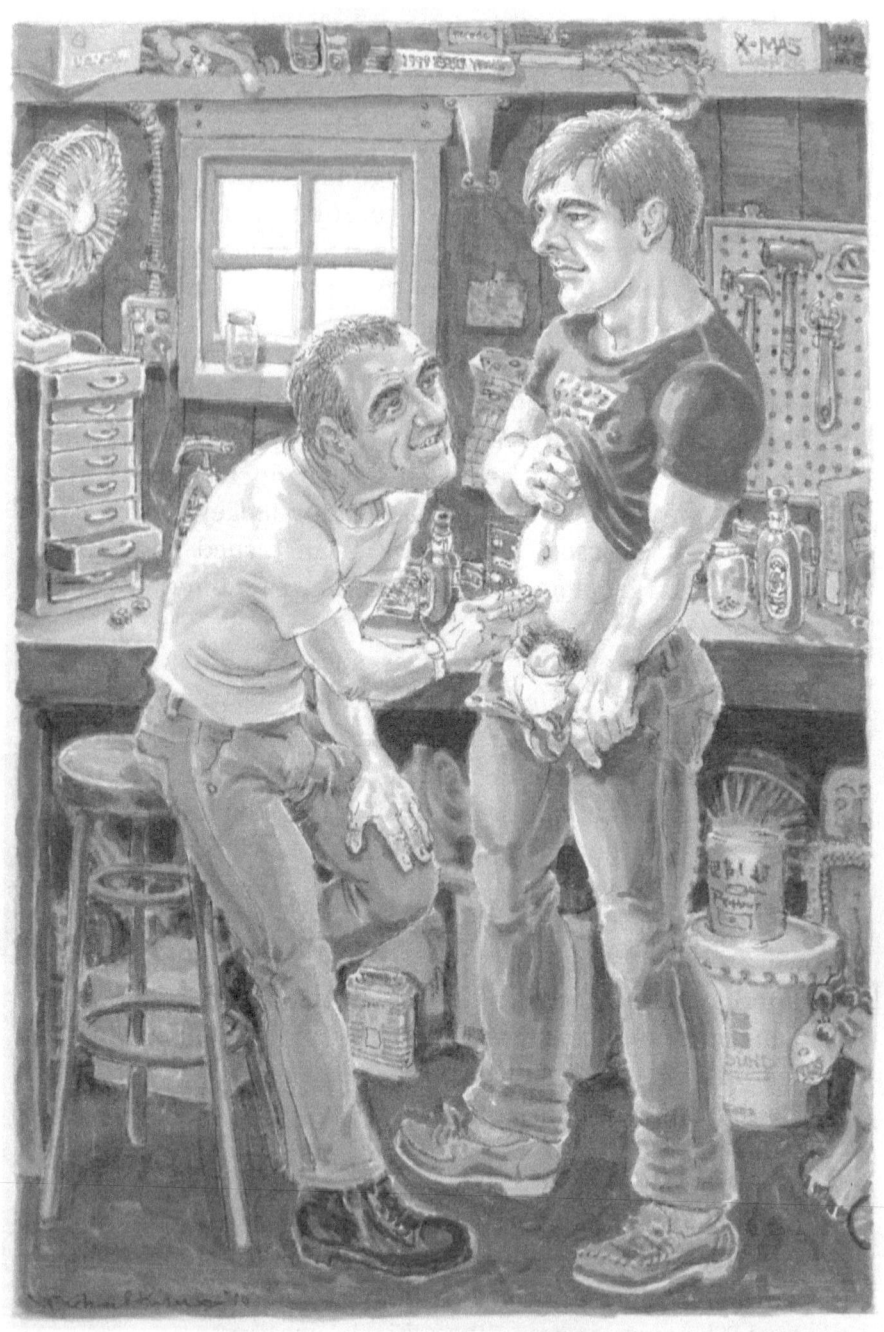

"So it's just between us?" Alan said.

"Well, I have to tell Dom, but don't worry. We're both discreet." Randy undid Alan's belt and took his pants and underwear down right there in the garage. His sweat-slicked cock bounded out, thick and long and eager. Had Alan ever done this before? Was he not getting any from his wife; was he legitimately desperate?

It didn't much matter. What mattered was his reaction when Randy held up his piece in his hand and whistled at the size and beauty of it.

"Amazing," Randy said, and Alan's sincere, unguarded smile took about fifteen years off of his face.

Randy took the prick into his mouth, getting his knees as comfortable as he could on the cement floor, taking it down to the root. He buried his nose in the young husband's dewy pubic bush, inhaling his scent. Alan rested a hand on the back of Randy's head, getting more aggressive as his orgasm approached. As he got close he grasped Randy's head with both hands, fucking his willing mouth and throat.

"Fuck man, I'm gonna cum," he said. Randy groaned in response, concentrating on keeping his throat relaxed for the inevitable. Alan pumped fast and furious as the cum began shooting out of his dick and filling Randy's throat. Randy struggled to swallow it all.

Not a whole lot had changed in their encounters since then. Alan liked head, specifically head from Randy. He avoided coming over when Dom's truck was in the driveway. Dom didn't care, because Alan wasn't really his type. With some exceptions, Dom liked his boys-on-the-side cute, young, and bubble-butted.

Alan didn't come by their house often—the stars pretty much had to align. His wife had taken the kids to their grandmothers. Or she was working late and the kids were at a friend's place. That sort of thing.

He'd knock on the back door, expectant and anxious, his eight-inch wonder already half-hard and swinging in his Dockers. He didn't reciprocate but Randy didn't much mind.

He'd leave with a smile on his face, having gotten what he needed, which wasn't only an orgasm. It was a certain amount of worship, and a reminder of what it felt like to be desired.

On the flip side of this was Jim Cunkleman, who'd first knocked on Dom and Randy's back door over fifteen years ago. Jim was well aware of what he had and didn't beat around the bush.

"Just moved in down the street and wanted to introduce myself," he said, all butch and cocky swagger. Dom and Randy invited him into the kitchen and offered him a cup of coffee. Jim was a Groom native, and was newly married. Randy had seen the two of them moving in—she was pretty and pregnant. He was strapping, red-headed, and hot as hell. "I've known about you guys for a long time," he said with a smirk on his red-bearded face.

"Is that so?" Dom said. "What have you known?"

"Oh, I just heard you were friendly is all," he said, leaning his elbows against their counter and letting his shirt ride up his belly.

"That usually scares guys off," Randy said, looking blatantly at Jim's engorged crotch.

"Not me," Jim said, keeping a sly eye on Randy as he adjusted his prick. "I like meeting new people." A few insinuations later Dom and Randy were kneeling on the linoleum and giving him head from each end.

It didn't usually happen that easily. Jim was something of a special case. Randy learned he was thirty-one, and had been living in the city for the past ten years before he'd knocked up his wife and moved back to Groom. Now, just as she was ready to nest, he was compelled to spread his seed far and wide. That was why Jim started showing up at their back door several times a week. He was fulfilling his biological role. He was horny by God's design.

One night when the three of them were playing poker Jim raised the stakes and put everybody's asses on the line. Of course he'd won.

"You cheated," Dom said. Randy had sensed the same thing. But neither of them could figure out how he'd done it, and of course it didn't matter.

"A bet's a bet," Jim said, sitting back in his chair. He'd got his two gay friends lubed and up ready, right next to each other on the living room floor, and he'd taken turns sticking it to both of them. They'd all blown at least one load a piece by the time that night was through.

Unlike other past and present down-low patrons of the Homo Hut, Jim didn't shy away from them on the street. He was always respectful, even if he was fucking their asses and calling them cockwhores behind closed doors.

"Does she know you come over here?" Randy asked him once.

"Yeah she does. It's poker night, I tell her."

"Do you think she...knows-knows?" Jim scratched his chin, thinking.

"I suppose she must on some level," he said. "But I think as long as I keep it to myself, she doesn't care."

"Do you guys have sex?" Dom asked.

"You kidding me? More than we ever have. But I like you guys, I really do. There's something to be said for people who don't fit in with the crowd. There's less bullshit."

So Jim was a fuck buddy but he also became a friend, and he stayed that way even during his messy divorce and the years when he drank too much. He'd stopped coming around for a while as he was drying out, but when he did return he was hornier than ever.

"I suppose I wasn't meant for married life. I got too much love to spread around," he said. He shocked them both that time

11

by stripping naked and laying face-down on the couch, his fine firm butt offered up to them both.

"Turnabout is fair play," he said over his shoulder. "With all the pounding I've been giving you two over the years, you should have a chance to knock off a piece of your own."

⌗

That was the kind of guy Jim Cunkleman was, easy and free. Which was a marked contrast to the kid who now stood before Randy, a kid who kept having to jerk back his straying eyes like they were leashed dogs nosing in the wrong yard.

It wasn't the time, however, to consider the implications.

"C'mon, I'm taking you home," Randy said, and he threw on some clothes. Dan didn't protest or try to flee—just trailed sullenly and wordlessly behind Randy for two blocks.

Randy rang the doorbell and Dan's dad answered the door. That was when Randy realized why the kid didn't seem panicked over giving his parents a late-night wake-up call.

Dan's dad—Tom Frye—stood there in his boxer briefs, the annoyance on his face only increasing when he saw that it was Randy standing there next to his son. Tom Frye was a ripped stud who *always* had a nauseous look reserved for the town fags.

"Morning," Randy said, smiling big and chancing a glance at Tom's semi-nude body—the rounded shoulders, massive, slab-like pecs and tight stomach covered in a brush of dark hair. The bulge in his black boxer briefs was a little disappointing, Randy thought, though nothing to scoff at when you considered the total package.

Randy handed Tom the spray paint can. "I caught your son vandalizing my house just a bit ago." Tom took the paint can, looked at it and looked back to Randy. Randy had every

12

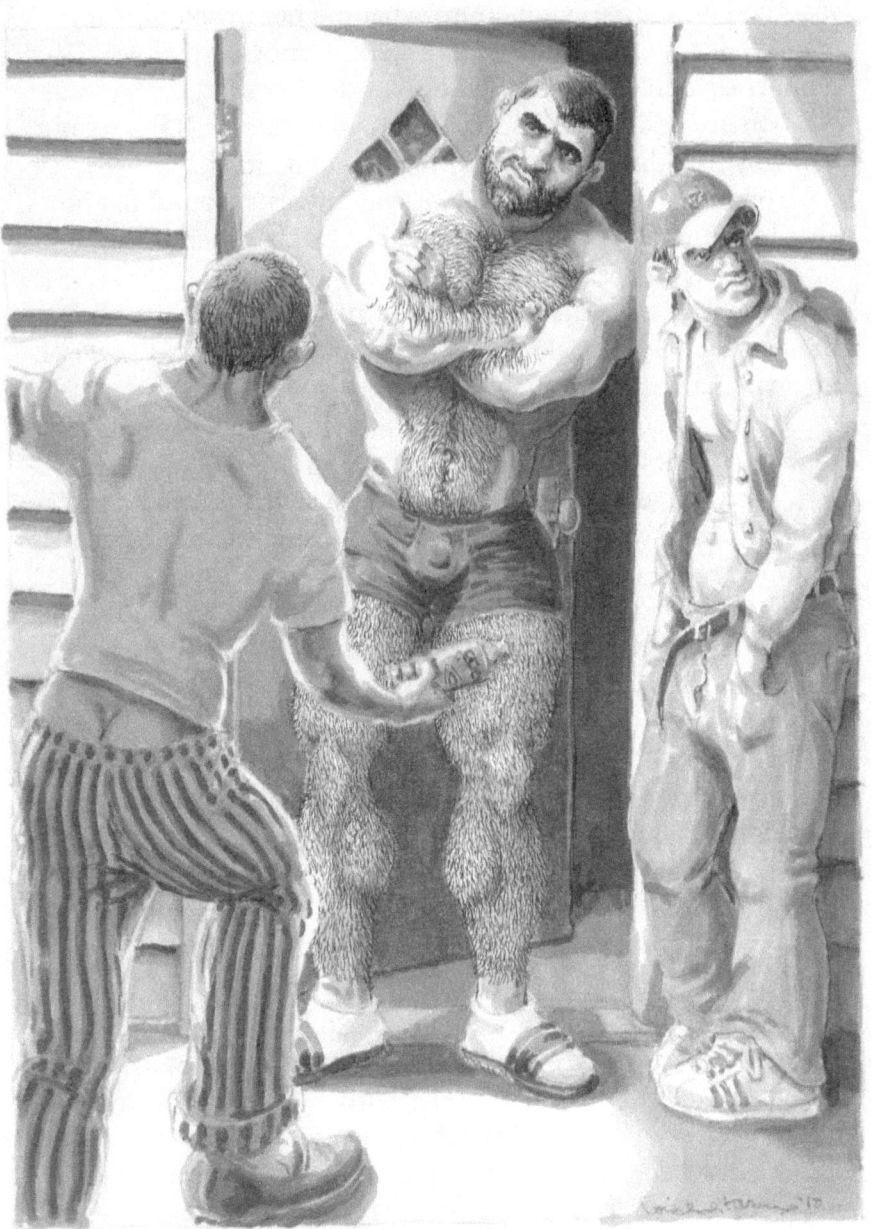

expectation that the tree was preparing to defend its fruit, but just then Mrs. Frye came up from behind her husband.

"What's going on?" she asked. Randy explained. Her embarrassment was immediate.

"Oh my God, I am so sorry," she said to Randy. "I'll have him come by first thing tomorrow morning to fix it."

Tom didn't say anything—just put an arm around his boy's shoulder and ushered him inside, not doing much to hide the pride he felt for his not-gay son.

At least I got to see Tom Frye in his underwear, Randy thought as he got back in bed. It almost atoned for the whole inconvenience.

He was pretty surprised when Dan did, in fact, show up later that day, paint brush in hand.

"My mom made me come back," Dan said, his face a mixture of humiliation and loathing. Randy almost felt bad for the little shit.

They drove to the hardware store. While they were waiting for the paint to mix, Jim Cunkleman came up from behind Randy and goosed him.

"Jesus, you fucker," Randy said to Jim.

"You love it," Jim said with a widescreen grin. His shift at the hardware store (where he'd worked for the past five years) was almost done and he was feeling pretty good about it. "Buyin some paint, eh?" He nodded his head in greeting at Dan, who looked ready to flee in fear. Dan had obviously caught sight of Jim's prank. *He probably thinks I'm trying to induct him into some secret small-town fag network*, Randy thought.

"What you been up to?" Randy asked him.

"Oh you know, just working hard when I'm not with my girl. And even then I'm working pretty hard," he said, and shot Dan a wink. "I'll stop by one of these nights, though."

"Yeah I bet you will," Randy said, his ass loosening at the prospect. The confusion on Dan's face was priceless. *Some way to get your mind blown*, Randy thought, *in the paint aisle at the hardware store.*

"How do you know that guy?" Dan asked Randy on their way back from the hardware store.

"Aw, he's just a friend," Randy said. "Why?"

"Nothing. I was just wondering how he knows...you guys," Dan said. Randy rolled his eyes.

"You know us, obviously, or you wouldn't have known which house to paint your dumb-assed graffiti on, right?" Dan kept his gaze steadfastly out the passenger-side window.

When they got back Randy procured a drop cloth and let Dan work on his own. Randy was lying on the couch, watching *Days of Our Lives* and considering the strange case of the homophobic Frye men. Dan's mom had insisted on him coming back, but surely he could've gotten out of it *somehow*.

Then Randy must have drifted off, because the next thing he sensed was someone standing behind the couch. He raised his head, turned, and saw Dan looking over the couch at him, brush in hand, large rod tenting out the front of his cargo shorts.

"I'm done," Dan said. Randy sat up, turned toward the kid. Dan saw him looking at his boner but made no motion to cover himself up. It was too late. He was stripped bare before the older man, exposed, and he began to quiver. An eighteen year-old with a battle raging inside of him between mind and body.

Randy stood and went over to him. He put a hand on Dan's shoulder and pulled Dan toward him. Dan resisted at first, then fell into Randy. Randy held him close. The kid's boner was pressing up against his leg. How did something that was meant to make life and pleasure end up causing such pain?

"It's okay," Randy said, stroking Dan's back. "It's gonna be alright." Dan's whole body convulsed as he started to cry.

Then he heard a knock at the back door. Randy quickly considered the possibilities. Maybe Alan had cut out on his lunch break. Maybe Jim had stopped by on his way home from work.

It didn't really matter, Randy told himself. Either of them would have something to teach the kid.

3. The Carnival

A carnival appeared in Groom every July, transforming the Legion field beyond the railroad yard into a queasy menagerie of thrills and wonders. Brian could see it on the horizon from the far edge of his backyard, swirling with crazy multi-colors against the dark summer sky. His parents never took him until the last night, Saturday, so he'd watch it all week and listen to the distant screams of the invisible crowd.

It was the summer of his thirteenth birthday. On Saturday he walked with his parents through town and into the field. They gave him some money and tickets and went on their way. He went through the funhouse. There were weird things in dark corners, remnants of displays that had been abandoned. A carnie, his face like worn, folded sandpaper, leered at him on his way out. Who were these people, Brian wondered, these ghost people who were here one week and gone the next?

He got in line for the Gravitron; one of those rides where that spun you so fast you stuck to the wall. It was fashioned like a flying saucer, the exterior all cool silver and pulsing lights.

"You ever ride this before?"

Brian turned to see a boy about three or four years older than him standing behind him in line. He had bleach-blond hair and was wearing a shapeless black jacket over a wifebeater that draped his thin white frame. He brought a cigarette to his mouth and took a hit.

"Yeah, I rode it last year for the first time," Brian said.

"Alright. Just making sure," the boy said, and winked. Brian turned to look at the ride. He looked back at the boy. He wasn't scared.

"I'm gonna spin upside down," the boy said. People did that; waited until the ride pasted their bodies to the wall and then rotated themselves vertically. It was supposedly against the rules but the operator (pumping loud rock music from a white-lit booth in the center of the ride) always let you get away with it. The boy kept taking shaky hits from his cigarette and shuffling his feet.

They filed inside the dimly-lit interior of the ride. Brian stood with his back against one burgundy cushion and the blond boy took the cushion next to him. They didn't say anything as the ride sped up. Brian was taken away with the pure force of it as it melted him to the wall, everything blurring, Aerosmith blasting over the speakers. It was a shot of controlled danger. You could forget everything in there, not least of which was that a week ago, in the same space now occupied by the carnival, there'd been nothing but swaying weeds.

The ride slowed. The blond boy had never turned upside down. Brian was laughing and his eyes were teary from the wind flow; the boy was laughing too. He moved to leave and Brian went to follow him but the boy stopped. His coat pocket, containing his cigarettes, had been sucked into the crack between the cushions. He yanked it free.

"My cigarettes," he said, pulling the green and white pack from his pocket. Brian filed out behind him. The boy stopped just outside the ride and seemed to want Brian to stop to, so he did.

"Want a smoke?" the boy said, holding a cigarette out to him.

"I never have," Brian said.

"Want to try one?" Brian felt his stomach flip-flop.

"I don't want my parents to see."

"If you want we can go out into the field over there," he said, motioning to the dark expanse beyond the carnival. He tucked the cigarette behind his ear.

"Okay."

"My name's Abe," he said, holding out his hand.

"Brian."

"Let's go." He followed Abe. They went past the rides,

17

past the hidden guts of the carnival, stepping over thick black electrical cords in the beaten-down grass. The lights and sounds began to recede, and soon they were alone in the semi-dark. Abe stopped.

"This is good," he said. He took the cigarette from behind his ear and put it between his lips. He got a lighter from his jacket pocket and brought the flame up to the end. It caught fire, crackling red as he sucked in a drag. He took it from his lips and exhaled, a billow of smoke that evaporated in the night air. He held it out to Brian. Brian put it between his lips.

"Don't breathe in too much," Abe said. "Just kinda suck the smoke into your mouth and breathe in only a little." Brian tried it. It tasted noxious. There was a sharp tingle as the smoke touched his virgin lungs, but he didn't cough. He exhaled a small puff.

"There you go," Abe said, taking the cigarette and pulling a big drag. Brian felt his head change. It was a giddy feeling. He laughed a little.

"What?" Abe said.

"Nothing. Feels cool." What it felt like was how life could possibly be, like a dream, like freedom. He took another hit and coughed this time, but Abe didn't laugh at him.

"Where do you go to school?" Abe asked.

"Here. In Groom. What about you?"

"I dropped out. I came with my girlfriend." He seemed to want a response so Brian nodded. "My buddy too. I can't fucking find either of them. They probably went off to screw someplace." He took one last drag and flicked the butt out into the dark. "You know about screwing?"

"Yeah," Brian said.

"I bet you never even kissed anyone."

"No."

"You haven't?"

"This girl Lisa kissed me on the cheek."

"I'm talking about *really* kissing someone. With tongue and everything." Brian shook his head.

18

"You're missin out, little man," Abe said. Brian looked up at him. "Come here," he said, and stepped in front of Brian. He leaned down to him and put his lips next to Brian's lips, then touched and pressed them together. Brian kissed him. Abe's tongue writhed into his mouth, tasting bitter and hot like the cigarettes. Brian used his tongue too, and it slid against Abe's. It was a surging instant of electric contact; seconds stretched to the breaking point.

Abe broke the kiss.

"That's what it's like," he said, regaining his posture and smiling down at Brian. "Pretty nice, huh?" Brian nodded. He was spun.

"Just wait till you get a girl to do it," Abe said. "Just wait, you'll see." They headed back to the lights and noise of the carnival.

"You gonna find your parents alright?" Abe said at the edge.

"Yeah, I will."

"I'm gonna find my friends. You take care, little man. Walk around before you find your parents. Air yourself out so they can't smell it on you." He waved and then got lost in the crowd.

Brian walked around for a while just watching people and wondering if they could smell it on him or see that he was different now.

4. Mr. Weist When He's At Home

Mr. Weist was eating a ham sandwich when Jon entered his classroom. It embarrassed Jon for some reason, like he'd caught his teacher in an intimate act.

"Hey Jon," the teacher said, wiping the side of his mouth. "Shut the door, would ya?"

"Mrs. DeTola wanted me to give these to you," Jon said, handing his teacher a stack of envelopes. "She said she needs them back by next week."

Mrs. DeTola was the head administrator at Groom Senior High, and Jon volunteered in the office during fifth period every Wednesday. Jon was in agreement with his mom that it would look good on his college applications, but he still felt like a traitor.

He wondered if Mr. Weist thought as much. Mr. Weist was the type of teacher that every kid in school respected and looked forward to having. He taught modern history to juniors (like Jon) and a psychology elective for seniors. Underclassman would hear stories about the cool stuff you'd get to do with him, like a report on a band from the '60s and a field trip to the state mental hospital. He was also the wrestling coach, and he'd brought the team to more than one state championship.

Jon had a crush on him. He was older, of course, but he'd kept himself in brick-shithouse condition. He had a granite jaw and a goofy smile. Sometimes Jon attended wrestling matches just to watch his teacher (he looked good in a suit, not that the spandex-clad muscle boys writhing on each other detracted from the experience).

"Oh swell," Mr. Weist said, taking the envelopes from Jon and setting them next to his lunch. "Have a seat, buddy. Want a chip?"

"No thanks," Jon said.

"How's tricks?" Mr. Weist sat back in his chair. Jon was having difficulty averting his eyes from the v-neck in his teacher's sweater—he wasn't wearing an undershirt, and it was bulging with his mounds of tan cleavage. "I've seen you at some matches—you interested in trying out?"

"No...not really." His previously-concocted lie about covering the matches for the school newspaper had escaped him.

"Just enjoy wrestling?"

"Yeah...I guess so." Mr. Weist smiled big, his eyes looking right through Jon. Jon felt his face getting hot.

"That's good," Mr. Weist continued. He picked up his sandwich and took another bite. "Shame you don't want to try out, though. You got the build for it."

"Thanks. You think?"

"Absolutely. You're thin, but you've got definition."

"I'm not built like those guys."

"Ehh, it takes all kinds. We've got a few boys you'd match up with." Jon nodded, pleased. "Don't worry. I wouldn't expect you to handle these pipes," Mr. Weist said, raising his arm beside his head and flexing his bicep. "You know what I'm talking about Jon? Couldn't handle these guns, could ya?"

Jon managed a laugh. "No sir," he said.

"Go on," the teacher said, getting up from his chair. He went around his desk to Jon, pushing up the sleeve of his sweater until his exposed, pumped-up muscle was in front of Jon's face. "Feel it."

Jon's breath was having trouble catching up to his heart. He wrapped his hand around his history teacher's bicep and squeezed.

"I'm pumped, I know it," Mr. Weist said. He didn't move his arm and Jon didn't move his hand. "You like that, huh?" Jon half smiled.

Mr. Weist sat on the corner of his desk. His legs were open and the swollen mound in his khakis was obvious. Jon couldn't look away. He looked up at his teacher. There was an

21

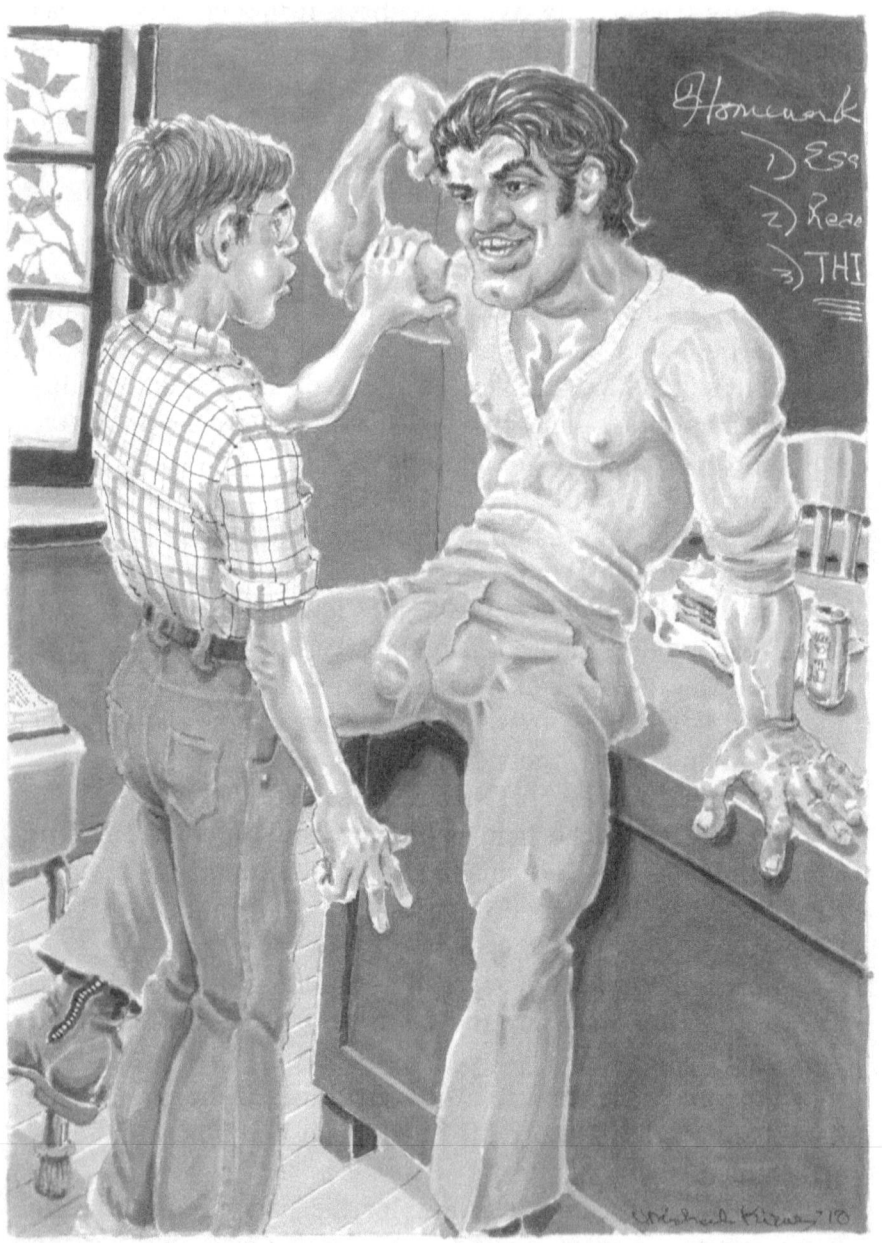

exhilarating moment when Jon realized that they were thinking the same thing.

Mr. Weist took Jon's hand and brought it to the front of his pants. "Like that too, dontcha?" he said.

It was a rhetorical question.

He suggested that Jon stop by his house later that night.

"It's on Brady Street," Mr. Weist began to explain, but Jon already knew. His teacher—unmarried—lived alone in a small yellow house three blocks up the hill from Jon. In moments of horny weakness Jon would stalk past, but the house had opaque curtains that were always shut. One Tuesday Jon stole his trash. He found an empty canister of protein powder and the wrapper from a Toblerone. It wasn't much but it was more than he'd had.

Once his teacher finished giving him the directions he grabbed Jon's crotch in his big man hand. "Mmmm," he said, kneading Jon's boner. "This'll be fun, right?"

"Uh-huh," Jon managed to say.

His teacher leaned close to his face. For a moment Jon thought he was going to kiss him.

"Try to wait at least until it's dark, and come to the back door," Mr. Weist whispered into his ear. "Maybe dress dark, too, so people can't see you."

❉

The rest of the day was a loss. He couldn't pay attention and none of it seemed to matter anyway. He took a shower when he got home and was too nervous to even get an erection. He forced down some food and after waiting for the sun to set, told his mom he was going out for a walk.

Mr. Weist opened the door wearing a pair of shorts and a tank top. His tan flesh was bulging out everywhere. He ushered Jon inside, scanning the backyard as if there were spies in the

23

bushes.

"My man," he said once Jon was safely in the kitchen. "You made it." Jon asked if he could use the bathroom. Mr. Weist showed him down the hall, Jon following his teacher's big butt with his eyes. He locked himself in the bathroom and tried to breathe normally.

When he got out Mr. Weist was in the kitchen eating cereal. Jon peeked into his living room. It was like a lost '70s bachelor pad—brown paneling, a lamp in the shape of an owl, a worn plaid couch.

"Want something to eat?" Mr. Weist said from the kitchen. He got up from his chair and approached Jon in the hall.

"No thanks, my mom made me dinner."

"Guess that's not much why you're here, anyway," the teacher said, planting his hand on the wall above Jon's head and leaning in to him. "Right?"

"I guess so."

"Are you a virgin?"

"No," Jon lied.

"Good," Mr. Weist said, smiling down at him. He put his other hand against the wall. "Go ahead and touch me if you want. Wherever you want." Jon hesitantly went for his teacher's forearms. He felt up his biceps and his bare, rounded shoulders. His skin, though aged, was taut over his beefy muscles. He was relaxed and accommodating as Jon caressed his pecs and thick stomach under his tank top.

"Take my shorts down," he instructed, and Jon crouched down. He grabbed the bottom of Mr. Weist's shorts and pulled. The elastic waist expanded around the teacher's hips then popped loose, falling to his feet.

There was a thick white strap around Mr. Weist's midsection—a jockstrap, Jon realized. The front pouch was bulging out cartoonishly.

Mr. Weist lifted each foot so Jon could remove his shorts. The teacher lifted one leg and propped his foot against the wall beside Jon. "Feel it," he said, and Jon wrapped his hands around

24

Mr. Weist's thick calf muscle, stroking upward to his smooth thigh, stopping when his fingers reached the edge of Mr. Weist's jock.

"You know you can feel that too," Mr. Weist said. Jon felt the scratchy fabric of his jock pouch, the firm, coiled-up snake underneath. "Mmmm," his teacher moaned.

The teacher turned around. The two tanned halves of his butt were framed by the white straps of his jock. Mr. Weist rested his arms and head against the wall, arching his back to present his ass to Jon. Jon caressed it like a globe.

"Slap it," Mr. Weist said. "Give it a nice smack." Jon did as told. The slap made a quiet echo in the hall. "Little bit harder," Mr. Weist said. "I like it." Jon used more force. Mr. Weist jumped but didn't seem phased. "Harder still," he said, and this time Jon really cracked it.

Mr. Weist jerked forward and moaned his approval. "That's the way, buster," he said.

He led Jon into the living room and set himself over his student's knee. "Spank me, buddy," Mr. Weist said, and the poor little virgin—who in all of his hours of fantasizing had never imagined such a scenario—did his best. The feel of Mr. Weist's jock-clad boner against his thighs was a nice enough motivation, and his teacher's hard and humpy butt was starting to grow on him. Mr. Weist squirmed and groaned, grinding his hard-on into the boy's lap as Jon let loose with a series of stinging slaps. Mr. Weist's buttcheeks got red and hot. Jon caressed the gooseflesh on his firm loaves before winding up with another smack.

When his teacher had gotten his fill of punishment he stood up. He grabbed Jon under his arms and lifted him up, setting his feet on the floor. Hungrily, the teacher stripped the boy down.

"Beautiful," he said, and used his mouth to devour Jon's skinny chest and stomach. Then he pushed him hard, so his body flung back on to the couch. "You're a hot little fucker, you know that?" he said, and stripped off his jock. Eight inches of thick boner bounced out, the head of it glazed with pre-cum.

"Ever sucked a dick before?" Mr. Weist asked.

"No," Jon said. His teacher sat back on the couch and issued Jon between his legs to begin his lesson.

He learned two things that night, in fact. The first was how enjoyable giving head could really be, especially when your beefy teacher was laid-back and patient and letting you enjoy his dick at your own pace. Jon even managed to make him cum, and at Mr. Weist's urging he tried a taste, licking at little off of his teacher's hairless sac.

The second was how good it felt getting head. His teacher's big hands roamed all over his body as he worked him over with his mouth, expertly suctioning the young man's cock in his hungry mouth with a relentless intensity. When his teacher's fingers roamed into his hairless butt crack he lost it. Mr. Weist swallowed every drop.

In light of this, it didn't matter so much that Mr. Weist had to scan the street from his living room window right before Jon left. It tarnished Jon's glow, just a little, but that wasn't a feeling he could rationalize. Obviously, what they were doing was wrong.

"Keep your head down until you get past the block," Mr. Weist said, lifting the hood on Jon's sweatshirt and covering his face with it. He squeezed Jon's cock through his jeans.

"See you in class tomorrow."

He tried to hold it inside but the temptation was too great. He told his best friend Tina on Sunday. Her eyes got big and she plied him for details.

"I guess I should tell you my own secret," Tina said, and proceeded to tell Jon how she'd fucked Mr. Simpson, the sophomore algebra teacher, at the Best Western last summer. The story began intriguingly, but the further along it went the less detail Tina was willing to convey.

"I only did it cause he bought us liquor and stuff," she said. "He's gross."

Mr. Weist called Jon out in front of the entire class that

26

That Friday, Mr. Weist saw to it that Jon had his first piece of ass.

"Just slide it in, buddy, no need to be gentle," Mr. Weist said, lying on his stomach in the bedroom, his legs apart and his lubed-up butthole winking at Jon.

If Jon was honest to himself he had to admit that he hadn't anticipated any of this. His fantasies about his teacher had involved a lot of soft-focus images of showering together, rubbing soapy bodies against one another—not riding his teacher's big butt until they both creamed. He saw himself making out with Mr. Weist after class—not getting the tar beat out of his ass with a ruler. But this was how it was, how Mr. Weist wanted it to be, and it wasn't like Jon had any room to complain. He was sixteen years old and adaptable as hell. He didn't last five minutes in his teacher's tight ass.

But he liked it even better that Mr. Weist made them dinner afterwards.

"It takes a real man to get fucked," Mr. Weist opined, flipping grilled cheese sandwiches in the pan. "People look down on it, like it turns you into a girl. Way I see it you gotta be strong, to take the pain and let it go."

"I'd like to try," Jon said. Mr. Weist chuckled.

"I bet you would," he said. He reached under the table and tweaked Jon's burgeoning boner. "All in good time." Jon didn't protest when they headed back to the bedroom and Mr. Weist got on his stomach again. Jon lasted longer this time.

Next Friday the tables were turned and Jon lost the last vestige of his virginity. Mr. Weist was patient and accommodating, lying back on the kitchen floor to let Jon straddle his strapping body. Jon braced himself on Mr. Weist's slab-like pecs, lowering his virgin butt on to Mr. Weist's pointed spear. He felt an exquisite pressure against his hole, like a thumb in the soft spot of an apple. Then it gave way and there was a sharp pain, but that passed and he inched downward until his butt was fully rested on Mr. Weist's pelvis. That was when Jon's cock started shooting spontaneously.

"Holy shit, kid," Mr. Weist said breathlessly as Jon showered him with cum. Mr. Weist's cock pulsed inside him and Jon realized he was losing it too.

"I couldn't help myself," Mr. Weist said afterward. They were getting dressed. Jon's ass was sore but already he felt different, like he'd passed through some mystic rite and would never be the same. "Just seeing you like that with my dick in your ass... it was too much." He tousled his hair. "You're a real good kid."

Jon felt very soft, like he was ready to cry. He wanted to grab on to this big man in front of him, to hold him and thank him, but that wasn't the way it was.

He took the long way home and stopped at the diner for pie. It was a busy night. He looked at all the people there—some as old as his grandparents. Most likely none of them were virgins. Like Jon, they all carried a secret life.

※

They'd planned it for a month. Jon had insisted. It went against the teacher's better judgment—the spanking he'd administered to Jon after class had been spontaneous, and dangerous. Yet he couldn't deny the appeal. He had Jon hide in the classroom supply closet while the building cleared out.

Once the coast was clear Mr. Weist let him out. He stripped Jon nude and had him sit in the front of the class as he gave a lesson on the Vietnam War. Halfway through the lesson Mr. Weist let his cock out of his pants—hard and bobbing—and continued the lecture.

When Jon got in trouble for not paying attention Mr. Weist made him get up on his desk and spread his ass. The teacher was pressing one thick finger to the boy's hole when they heard whistling coming from down the hall.

"Shit, it's Billy," Mr. Weist whispered. The custodian. The

teacher tucked his cock back into his pants. Instead of heading back to the closet, Jon scrambled under Mr. Weist's desk. Mr. Weist looked peeved but sat down at his desk, anyway, with Jon between his legs. The custodian knocked on the door.

"Quiet now," the teacher whispered to Jon.

"You still there Mr. W?" the custodian said.

"Yeah, Billy," Mr. Weist said. Jon heard the door open. His teacher's cock was still half-hard and laying to the left under his pants. Jon reached out to feel it. Mr. Weist's leg jerked but he didn't knock Jon's hand away. "Just grading some papers."

"Working late, are ya?" the custodian asked. Jon could hear him sweeping the floor. He slowly slid his teacher's zipper down and released his cock. He felt reckless. He almost wanted to get caught.

"Yep, no rest for the weary," Mr. Weist said, just before Jon went down on him whole-hog. The teacher's whole body tensed up.

"You ain't one to stay after hours, usually speaking, I mean," Billy said. Mr. Weist's cock was harder than hard and Jon could tell it wasn't going to take much to make him blow. He bobbed his head quickly, working his fist and mouth in tandem.

"Guess not," Mr. Weist said. His voice was strained. Jon heard the custodian stop sweeping.

"You alright there, Mr. W?"

"Yep, fine," Mr. Weist said. He shuffled some papers.

"Hmm." Billy continued sweeping. "Yeah, I never see you here round this time, but I guess it just adds to your mystery."

"Oh yeah?" Jon grabbed his teacher's nuts and held them tight. Mr. Weist drew up his knees and Jon knew he was passing the point of no return.

"That's what people say, you know," the custodian said. "Because you don't talk a whole lot about yourself I guess." Jon pulled on Mr. Weist's balls and that was it: the teacher was cumming, and Jon was swallowing it down, fresh from the source, in quick gulps, just like he'd learned. Mr. Weist maintained deep, even breaths. If Billy noticed anything he didn't say.

"I tell em it's none of their business," the custodian continued. "I tell em, 'Don Weist's a nice guy and that's all you need to know about him."

5. The Basement

Tom Frye descended the glossy green stairs to the basement of his old junior high school. This was not a dream.

When he dreamed of this basement it was night, the hallway dark but for light glowing from around a corner at the far end: the locker room where—at age eleven, his sexuality a swelling bud—he'd first gotten naked in front of other boys. He'd walk toward that awful fluorescent light, unable to stop himself, turned on and afraid, which was really the story of his subconscious life.

But, rich as Tom's dream life was, he didn't realize he had one. As far as he was concerned, he didn't dream at all.

It had been at least thirty years since he'd been in this old building. He felt uneasy as he reached the bottom of the stairs, but unsure of why. The hall was bright. It was daytime. There was an open door to his right and he walked into it.

The junior high had been closed for the past ten years before the owners decided to lease out a section of it to a local entrepreneur. They'd turned the old wood shop into a fitness center, and Tom had to admit, the place looked good—well-lit, cheery, with rows of nautilus and elliptical machines that were multiplied in a mirrored wall.

The only person there was a girl at a desk. She was friendly as she set up his membership.

"Where is the locker room?" Tom asked.

"Oh it's just down the hall," she said. Tom paused.

"You mean it's the old one?"

"Yeah, it's the original one. We fixed it up, though."

"Okay," Tom said, ignoring the anxious feeling in his stomach as stepped onto the treadmill and took off running.

Tom already had a membership at a gym outside of Deep Hollow, and he spent the majority of his free time there. His body was bangin, and not just for a guy in his early 40s with a wife and a teenaged son. His body was his greatest accomplishment.

When the gym opened in Groom he'd at first avoided it. But it was close—two blocks from his house—and his wife, Danielle, was always complaining that he spent too much time away from the house, so he'd relented.

After he'd been running for five minutes, a red-headed guy about Tom's age entered the gym. He winked at the desk girl and she grinned back. He climbed on the elliptical machine right next to Tom, nodding at him as he did. Tom didn't nod back.

By the time Tom had moved on to free weights, the red head (whose name was Jim Cunkleman) was doing yoga on the floor. Tom, standing stock-still as he bulked up his biceps, watched Jim bring himself into downward dog, his supple ass spreading wide underneath his sweat shorts. He was a fit guy, but in no way Tom's equal.

They finished their workouts at around the same time. Jim nodded to him again and smiled as they entered the locker room together.

The place looked almost exactly as Tom remembered. The only difference was that the showers had been renovated into three individual stalls instead of the old free-for-all. Tom took a locker and was dismayed when Jim took one a just a few lockers down from him.

"You do a hell of a job on yourself, bud," Jim said as they stripped.

"Thanks," Tom said. He turned his back to Jim as he lowered his shorts.

"I'm too damn lazy to make good of myself like you." Tom heard him shut the locker. He turned just in time to see Jim throwing his towel over his shoulder, his long, sweaty cock swinging from a thatch of auburn pubes, his butt perched out behind him as he sauntered toward the showers.

Tom hadn't realized his cock was swollen until he'd taken off his underpants. He wrapped a towel around himself and walked to the showers. Jim had taken the center stall, forcing Tom to enter one adjacent. He took the left side. Slipping off his towel and pulling back the curtain he found he'd raised a full-fledged boner. It bounced around as he soaped himself. Jim whistled as he showered. There was only a thin fiberglass wall between them, with open spaces above and below. Tom could see Jim's feet. He wrapped his hand around his soapy, half-hard cock, his heart racing.

"Hey chief," Jim said from the next stall. "Got any shampoo I can borrow?"

"Uh...yeah," Tom said. He held the bottle over the top of the stall. Nothing happened for a moment, then Jim took it.

"Thanks bud," he said. Tom soaped his chest slowly, every nerve ending in his body aware of the wet, naked guy lathering his hair next to him. He had to get rid of this boner. He tried to train his mind on awful things, shit and horror, but Jim interrupted.

"Got a hot date tonight," Jim said. Tom looked up—Jim was holding the bottle over the wall. Tom grabbed it. "Don't want to look like a greaseball. You hear me?"

"I'm married," Tom said.

"Wish that would've stopped me back in the day," Jim said, chuckling. Tom was finished, but was still harder than hard. "Met this girl at the bank, of all places," Jim continued. "Twenty-nine. Perky little tits. Sweet ass..." He gave a little growl. Tom was quiet. He'd started stroking himself again, his ears fully focused on the next stall. Up until now, the sound of the spray had varied, occasionally making a hollow splash against the plastic curtain. Now it was steady—was the guy standing still? Doing what?

Then he heard it—maybe. A slight, guttural grunt. Maybe even the wet squish of the guy jerking his dick, just like Tom was, but it could have been his ears playing tricks on him. He kept still and quiet, stroking lightly as the shower standoff ensued.

Tom decided to test something. He audibly released his breath.

Jim sniffed. Tom's heart raced. Another little grunt came

34

from Jim's stall. Tom's heart was beating so hard it hurt his throat; all his senses were prickling and alert. He let out his breath again and tried to put a little sound in it this time, it came out like a whimper.

Then from the next stall: "Mmmmm, fuck yeah." It was quiet enough, like the guy was saying it to himself, but there was no doubt about it now—he was jerking off. Tom stroked lightly—a slight breeze would've been a threat at this point.

"Feel good, buddy?" Jim said in a low but clear voice. It made Tom jump. "Yeah, man" Jim said, his foot coming closer to the stall divide as if he was widening his stance. It was all happening so fast. Tom was still stroking despite himself.

"Fuck yeah, I'm gonna cum," Jim said. "Oh shit. Ah! Ah!" That was all it took for Tom and he was shooting off too, his sperm splattering in thick slashes against the shower curtain and floor. He was trying modulate his breath, but his neighbor was going all out.

"Phew!" Jim said after a minute, and it came out like a laugh. Tom listened to him turn off the water and pull back the curtain. Tom used his hands to wash his cum off the curtain, his toe to break up the wad and send it down the drain. How had this happened? He waited as long as he could, hoping the guy would be gone when he came out.

But Jim was still there, looking in the mirror, combing his hair with his fingers. He looked at Tom's reflection and smiled.

"Nothin like taking a load off, huh chief?" Jim said. Tom walked past him to the lockers. He almost wanted to punch the guy.

Tom barely slept that night. His mind was overrun with memories he'd tried to suppress, like when he was eight and his friend had taken him into the woods and shown him some things. Or when he was at his high school buddy's house when his parents weren't home and they'd gotten carried away. All of it was ages ago, a wife and a kid ago, so why couldn't he let it go?

He went back to the Groom gym the next day, telling himself that it was only because he'd spent the money on a membership.

35

One more month and that was that.

Jim was there, of course—besides the girl at the desk, he was the only other person there. He was running on the treadmill, and when he spotted Tom he gave him a wide grin. Just like with the showers, Jim had taken the machine in the middle of the three, so Tom couldn't avoid taking the treadmill next to his.

"Evening, bud," Jim said. Tom climbed on the machine and Jim held out his sweaty hand. "We haven't met properly yet. I'm Jim Cunkleman."

"Tom Frye," Tom said, reluctantly taking his hand.

"I think you were a couple years ahead of me in school."

"Maybe," Tom said, cuing up the treadmill.

"Look a lot bigger than you did back then," Jim said. Tom shrugged, ran.

⊞

Jim kept his mouth shut for the rest of the workout. It was obvious to him that the guy was hung up, but then so were most people. Jim hadn't spent more than five minutes thinking about what they'd done in the showers yesterday—and even then it was merely to appreciate that he hadn't gone out on his date with a loaded gun.

The date had gone well, too. Her name was Sara Jolley. They'd had dinner at Touch of Class but, surprisingly, it had turned out to be formality for the both of them. Jim laid on the flirtation and Sara shoveled it right back. They skipped dessert and went back to Jim's house with a six pack, where they fucked like rabbits until night turned into morning.

Jim hit the shower and was heading out of the building when he got a call on his cell phone. He stopped outside the doors of the junior high and answered it. It was Sara.

"Are you still at your mom's place?" he asked.

36

"Yeah. Looks like I'm spending the goddamn night. I wish you were here right now though. I'm so horny," she said.

"Where are you?" Jim said, feeling his cock stir. He rested his back against the brick wall of the building. Gnats buzzed around the light above his head.

"I'm in my old bedroom. Everybody else is downstairs. Where are you?"

"Outside the gym," he said.

"I can't stop thinking about you," she said. "My panties are already wet. I'm putting my hand down there now."

"Jesus," Jim said in a whisper.

"My clit is hard. Oh Christ I'm so *wet...*"

"Jesus," he said again. He put his hand in his pocket and felt the head of his hard cock. "I'm wet too."

"I wish I was there to lick it off you—*shit*—" Over the phone Jim heard a knock then a voice: "*Sara, are you in there?*"

"Jesus Christ," Sara whispered. "*Yeah, I'm here!*" she called out. Then to Jim: "I'm sorry babe. We'll do this later?"

"Yeah," Jim said, the word sounding foreign and flat coming from his lust-flooded head.

"Call you later," she said, and hung up. He stood there for a minute, caught his breath. Then Tom came through the doors. He was visibly startled to see that Jim was still around.

"Hey there," Jim said, flipping shut his phone. He took a deep breath. "Headed home?"

"Yep," Tom said, clutching the strap of his bag over his shoulder. He started to turn away, but hesitated. He pretended to look for something in his gym bag.

"Want to drive around with me and drink some beer?" Jim said. "I know it sorta goes against all we've been doing, working out and all."

Tom looked up from his gym bag, at Jim. This was what he'd been waiting for after all, wasn't it? What he'd been hoping for and fearing at the same time?

He nodded slowly, dreamily.

"Well c'mon then," Jim said, fairly surprised that the guy

had agreed to go along with him. He'd only been thinking that he didn't feel like going home, and that jacking off wasn't going to quell the fire that Sara had lit in him with her phone call. Driving around and drinking some beer seemed like a good option. Maybe they'd park somewhere and jack each other off.

They went around the back of the building where their cars were parked.

"Alright if we take my truck?" Jim suggested. Tom nodded, giving him only the briefest glance.

They stopped to get a six pack. As soon as they rolled into the parking lot, Tom sunk down in his seat. Jim went inside the store and Tom considered making a run for it right then and there, but Jim was back before he could take any action.

Jim drove them to a field off of Falling Run Road, where he parked and shut off the headlights. His face glowed green from the dashboard lights as he handed a beer to Tom and they cracked them open.

"I've been here before," Tom said. He took another gulp from the beer and felt a warmth in his stomach that began to spread to the rest of his body. "Back in high school. I came here with my girlfriend."

"I think a lot of us came here with our girlfriends," Jim said with a grin. Tom grinned too. What he hadn't said was that the girlfriend had been his only girlfriend, later to become his wife, and that the sex they'd had in her mother's Buick had felt like the beginning of the end.

The stereo played classic rock in low tones. Tom dared a glance at his companion. They were doing something normal, weren't they? Two guys hanging out drinking some beer.

"I come out here when I need to relax...take a load off, you know?" Jim said, looking at Tom. Tom's heart quickened.

"So what do you say?" Jim said, his eyes still on Tom. He cupped the bulge in his jeans. "We both know what we were doing yesterday, right? It was alright, right? So we'll do it again, 'cept this time without a damn wall between us." He massaged his swollen crotch and Tom's eyes followed every movement. "Look," Jim said, unbuttoning his jeans. He grasped the zipper pull and undid it slowly. He wasn't wearing any underwear. He hauled out his dick which was thick and already wet at the tip. "See how horny I am?"

Jim pulled his pants down the rest of the way till they were around his ankles. He sat for a moment letting Tom gaze at his cock. It pulsed. A drop of pre-jizz emerged from the tip.

"Ain't you gonna join me?" Jim said. "You look like you're ready," he added, glancing at Tom's lap. Tom was wearing a pair of basketball shorts and the rod he'd thrown was obvious. Tom took his eyes away from Jim's cock and looked down in his own lap. Seemingly dismayed by his erection, he looked sullenly out the window.

Jim took a deep breath and a drink of beer. He thought of saying *How about you close your eyes and I'll close mine and we'll pretend we're in the damn shower again*, but he didn't. He reached down and rested his hand on the rod in Tom's lap. Tom's chest began to rise and fall, rapidly. He took his eyes away from the window and looked at Jim's hand.

"Now that feels like a nice cock," Jim said, already going for the guy's waistband. Tom raised his butt off of the seat as Jim pulled off his shorts, revealing Tom's black briefs and hard, hairy thighs. "Let's take a look," Jim said, and tucked Tom's briefs under his smooth nuts. Tom's cock bobbed out. It didn't matter so much to Jim what it looked like; the important thing was that it was hard and ready to roll. Jim gave it a couple strokes. "It's beautiful, buddy. You're pre-cummin just as much as I am," he said, and shifted his attention to his own cock. He swiped a finger over the head of his dick, gathering the glob of pre-cum on his fingertip.

"Ever try your own stuff?" he said, and popped it in his mouth. "Mmmm." He stroked his cock from the base to the tip until another drop emerged. He got it on his finger. "Here," he said, and brought it to Tom's mouth. Tom took the calloused finger between his lips and licked it clean. "Like it?" Tom nodded. Jim served him up another helping. "You can have all you want," he said, nodding to his lap.

This is it, Tom thought. He leaned down, letting the warm beery feeling in his gut guide him. Jim's cock smelled earthy, like mossy cum and soap. He took it in his mouth, swiping his tongue against the head, then went lower and lower. It didn't make him choke. He was surprised to find Jim's balls resting against his chin. They were still damp from his shower.

"God, yeah, man," Jim groaned. Tom's cock throbbed thoughtlessly between his legs as he went for a second pass. Jim took another drink of beer as Tom bobbed his head in his lap. It felt amazing, but he couldn't stop feeling like he'd taken the guy too far. He gently pulled Tom off of him.

"Let's see you," he said, and took off Tom's shirt. He ran his hands over Tom's rigidly-defined muscles, found them sort of entrancing. Over his hairy chest, down his tight stomach, and finally around Tom's prick. He stuck his hands under Tom's thighs as he leaned down and took the guy's cock in his mouth. Tom's legs shuddered as Jim sucked him. It was something of an inexpert blowjob—he'd never been much of a cocksucker—but Jim wanted to please the guy. He cupped Tom's nuts in his hand, sliding his finger underneath them until he felt the wrinkled folds of Tom's asshole.

Bingo. Tom lifted off of his seat, and when he settled back in Jim's finger was still there, pressed to his smooth, puckered hole. Jim didn't let up—he gently massaged around it until Tom began to relax. He put more pressure on it until the tip of his finger sunk inside. He was thinking it felt hot and tight and was starting to get the enticing idea that he was going to get to stick his cock in there when Tom flooded his mouth with cum.

Unexpected, but Jim managed to adjust, swallowing like a

40

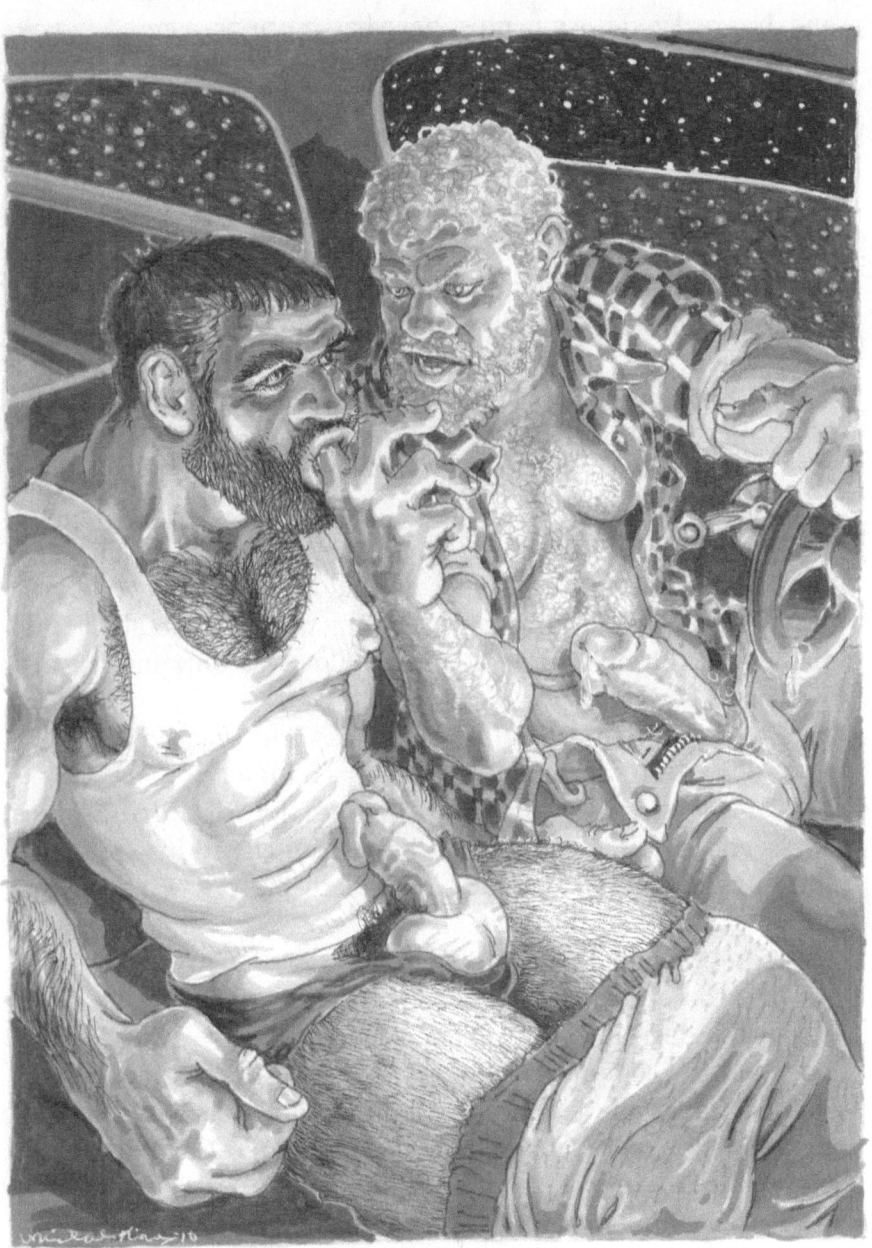

good buddy should. It went quickly and the cum was watery, and Jim realized the guy must have had a pre-orgasm.

"Damn, bud," he said, coming off of Tom's dick.

"Sorry," Tom said.

"Don't apologize. You taste great. Just took me by surprise is all." He still had his finger in Tom's hole. He wiggled it in a bit more and Tom's eyes rolled back in his head. "You like that? Here bud, let me give you a thrill." He lifted Tom's ankles and Tom fell back against the door of the car. Jim raised Tom's legs, exposing and spreading the guy's big muscle butt. He got down and licked Tom's ass from stem to stern in one long swipe, making contact with his hole just briefly.

"I like eatin ass," Jim said, and speared his tongue against Tom's hole. Tom's breath came in heaving grunts. Jim got him to hold his own ankles as he got Tom's hole wet and sloppy. He slipped a finger back inside. "Gripping me like a fuckin vice, man," Jim said. With his finger he could feel the beat of Tom's heart pulsing inside his asshole. The guy was all ass, really. He'd managed to crack him open and now he was bursting out all over like a goddamn piñata.

He took his finger out of Tom's ass and reached into the glove box. Tom watched him pull out a condom.

"Let's go outside," Jim said. Tom didn't move. Jim took his finger and slid it back in Tom's hole. Tom closed his eyes and Jim fingered him, in and out, slow, steady pumps. "I'll fuck you outside," Jim said.

"Can't we do it in here?" Tom said.

"It's too cramped in here. There ain't anybody out there except the deer and raccoons and they don't give a shit." Tom looked at the roof of the truck. He concentrated on the feeling of Jim's finger and found himself nodding. It was like a horror movie where you're screaming *"Don't go in there!"* but of course it's pointless.

Jim led him to a tree. They didn't have any lube so Jim put Tom on his knees in the high grass and had him suck his condomed cock until it was wet and sloppy. Then he braced

Tom against the tree and ate him out some more.

He stood and rested his cock against Tom's rounded rear. Tom braced himself. When Jim's cockhead found his hole and Jim managed to work it inside, he found the initial pain to be harsh but not unendurable. Jim was patient.

"Damn bud," he said, sliding some more inside. "So fucking tight." He shoved his cock in all the way and ran his hands up Tom's chest, tweaking his nipples. He started fucking him, slowly, savoring it. His dick was splitting Tom's muscled butt into two halves. He started to give Tom the reach around. Tom, his broad back to Jim, turned his head to Jim.

"Don't. You'll make me cum," he said.

"That's the idea, bud," Jim said. He fucked him harder. Tom grabbed the tree, felt the bark under his hands. Everything seemed to come at him at once. The warm wind on his nude body. The fireflies winking on and off in the distance. He heard the train whistle, low and far away.

"I'm really going to cum," Tom said.

"I ain't even touching you anymore," Jim said, but Tom barely heard him.

"Oh fuck! Fuck me!" he cried as his load shot out, his ass pulsing against the monstrous thing invading it. His load shot against the trunk of the tree where it pooled in the crevices of the bark.

Jim felt it happening, felt Tom's insides pulsing around his cock. He waited until Tom was done before he pulled out and yanked off the condom. He wanted nothing more at that moment then to shoot his load all over this beautiful guy's back and butt, and that was what he did. With one hand on Tom's shoulders he held his hose and let loose, sending his cum down Tom's arched back where it drizzled down the deep crevice of his ass crack. He slapped his cock against Tom's hard ass cheeks as he came down.

"Christ," he said with a laugh. Tom stood up. "Feel good for you buddy?" Jim said.

Tom didn't turn around. Regret was flooding the places

43

desire had just left. "Take me back to my car, please," he said.

And so Jim did. He respected Tom's unspoken wish for silence, even if he didn't understand it. And as Tom secreted the night's experience into dank, unseen places, Jim steered the truck along the winding road, regarded the moonlit pastures beyond. He saw these fields in his dreams sometimes, lush green hills that rolled off toward the horizon, and there was no reason he couldn't fly over them, follow their easy loping surfaces into the sunset.

6. The Opera House

Britt and Cody had rules, but you couldn't talk about them and they were always changing. This made things confusing.

Take cum, for example. They were trading hands not long after they first started beating off together. And though it was understood that they try to cum at the same time, Britt had inwardly decided that getting Cody's cum on his hand was gross. So when orgasms approached, it was hands to one's self.

Then one night it wasn't. They were lying on the living room carpet jacking each other off, their heads up against the industrial cable spool they used for a coffee table and their feet dipping under the fabric flap at the bottom of the busted easy chair. Their slim naked sides collided in little electric volts of contact, but all in all it was a typical scene at 3 a.m. in their shared apartment in the rural town of Groom, Pennsylvania. There was a newly purchased and half-killed case of Keystone beer in the fridge and a girl was being double-penetrated on the TV.

Then their heads turned and their lips touched, and the next thing Britt knew Cody was making out with him. Making out was questionable behavior, though they'd done it before—but only because their TV was broken and they couldn't watch porn, and making out helped Britt get hard. By some miracle of the male animal mind, kissing had become purely functional.

But Britt's mom had bought them a new TV a week ago, so that excuse was gone. Fortunately they'd been doing tequila shots earlier that day and Cody had eaten the worm, so maybe that forgave it, and Britt kissed right back as they writhed around, fists working overtime. Cody's tongue slid softly between Britt's lips, drawing their orgasms closer.

Thus in the space of a minute two rules had been tested—

Britt was cumming and Cody was cumming and it was streaming all over their respective hands. As they broke apart and wiped up Britt figured it wasn't the end of the world—they were using the same crusty, bleach-spotted towel they'd been sharing for weeks now anyway, so what was the difference?

One lazy Sunday morning not long after, Britt (who'd woken up rock-hard, having had an intense and wholly-forgotten dream about Cody) shot a streaming rope of cum right across the golden dusting of hair on Cody's chest. Cody, (a towhead with a big cock that more than made up for his lack of self-confidence) started cumming too, and feeling turnabout was fair play he arched his hips upward and blew jizz onto Britt's bony pelvis. They'd chided each other about it afterward, then that night did it deliberately, both of them directing their spewing cocks onto each other's bodies in a mock display of maliciousness.

They progressed to eating their own loads, Britt one night throwing his legs up over his head with a bold smile and a devious look in his heavy-lidded eyes. He sent several creamy shots of cum sailing into his open mouth, some of it oozing down his sparsely stubbled face; then made a show of licking his lips. Cody was appropriately shocked and fake-appalled, but next time Britt "talked him into doing it" too. Soon they were regularly blasting in their own mouths, having drummed up some nonsense about how it was criminal to "waste it" and that chicks who spit were dumb cunts who didn't deserve their cocks anyway.

Not that any girls were banging down their door. Or that they necessarily wanted them to.

❊

So. How had they progressed to eating each other's cum? Oral sex was a huge no-no, and admitting an interest in it would have been tantamount to gaily gadding about with a frilly pink parasol in hand.

The lame and tortured excuse for a catalyst had been Britt's drunken shit-talking about how "*My load tastes better than yours.*" What a con, they both knew it, but Cody took the bait like a good little guppy.

"Like you'd know," he said. They were standing in the kitchen, using one hand to suck down cigarettes and the other to tweak their half-hard dicks through their boxers.

"Whatever, dude. You know it tastes better if you eat, like, vegetables and shit, and I get those salads at McDonald's all the time," said Britt.

"My cum tastes fine," Cody said, dropping the butt of his cigarette in a beer can.

"So put your money where your mouth is. Or your mouth where my cock is," Britt said.

"Fuck you."

"You always scrunch up your face when you eat yours!" Britt said. By now he'd thrown a huge rod. It was exceptional when they found the language to talk about it, when they drew it out to the edge.

"That's cause I'm cumming. I'm like, overwhelmed."

"Bullshit," Britt said, and it was, all of it was, but when it led where it led —Britt acquiescing to his own challenge, licking Cody's load off of his slender stomach to compare and doing it hungrily ("How is it?" Cody asked. "Nasty," Britt said after he'd eaten every drop. "Told you"), then Britt jacking himself off and Cody sucking the cum off of Britt's fingers, one by one till they were clean—how could you deny it? It was filthy, and it was hot.

But you weren't allowed to say that. Once Cody had, and Britt shot him a withering look that dropped Cody's stomach like a stone in a well. It took a whole day of strained cohabitation before they were doing it again.

Life was momentary for Britt Laney and Cody Jackson. One moment they were smoking a joint of dirt weed they'd scraped together from errant baggies, the next they were shoving garage tools up their asses. (That was thanks to Britt, who'd broken the ass-ice after months of them doing all they could to avoid it.)

Momentary because the boys, both nineteen, were away from home for the first time and enjoying every minute of their independence.

They'd met after their first semester at VyoTech, the local technical school where they were studying to become auto mechanics. By spring they had moved into a unit in the Opera House on Main Street. The Opera House had been just that in Groom's late nineteenth-century heyday, when the river and railroad between Pittsburgh and Philadelphia had sent industry and the town's population booming. At some point the block building was gutted and sectioned off into apartments that hadn't been renovated since 1962, but who cared when you were paying $350 a month for a two-bedroom place? Not the landlords, that was for sure.

They were friends—best friends, and that was the extent to which they could admit to their relationship. They knew what faggots were and knew that they weren't faggots. There *were* faggots in town; older guys, boyfriends apparently, who owned a house on Spring Street—Clitter Schreve, their townie friend and fellow gearhead, had pointed it out.

At first Britt had thrown a lot of fag-talk around, but that ebbed, mainly because Cody didn't play up to it. Cody may have been confused but as far as he was concerned what he and Britt did was their business, and what the faggots did was theirs. As long as Britt thought the 'twain should never meet, he'd think the same.

It got a little tricky once they started blowing each other. It began as a natural progression from feeding each other loads of cum—Cody would sit on Britt's scrawny chest, his dick close to Britt's open lips, and it was only natural that his cock head should bump against them. So Britt started wrapping his lips around the head of Cody's cock—made it easier to catch his cum, anyway, and it wasn't like you were chugging a cock past your gag reflex like some gutter whore.

Cody did it in turn, just like he did anything once Britt implicitly allowed it. They found it felt even better when the other used his tongue a little, nursing the head between his lips like it was a nipple or a lollipop. Then Britt went for broke and slid his mouth all the way down Cody's big dick, and it was cool, no big deal —so Cody began taking all of Britt's small one.

The rules regarding this were subtle and amorphous. It was okay to swallow a dick the whole way every once in a while, but bobbing the knob too much was suspect. Head movements were to be kept to a minimum. All of this was under the guise of eating each other's loads, so if you were using your mouth to help that along, fine. If you were sucking to suck it was not fine.

Their asses were the demarcation point, the event horizon. But from the beginning their buttholes were engaged, squinching and releasing so exquisitely as surges of pleasure swarmed through their bodies. The act of throwing their legs over their heads, warm holes exposed to the cool air, had been an unspoken but key element to what made the self-facials so exciting.

It happened one night after they'd been doing beer bongs in their apartment with Clitter Schreve and another townie, who both eventually left to find crank. Britt and Cody fell into an old-school joint jerk-off, stroking each other's cocks on the living room floor with big drunken smiles on their faces, the newly quiet apartment offering a giddy sense of promise and sexual release.

Cody had expected the usual—maybe some making out and then quasi-blowjobs. But Britt suddenly let go of Cody's dick and began tending to himself, intently watching the porno on the TV. Cody got worried, wondering if he'd crossed some invisible line.

But something was up—Britt was beating off and making it last, drawing it out longer and longer. Cody's back started to hurt from leaning against the couch, so he hoisted himself up on to it. That was when Britt swung his legs over his head, almost as if he'd been waiting for Cody to move, to give him an aerial view of his spread-wide ass.

"Man, I can't wait to feed myself a load, you know?" Britt said. He ran his hands up and down his back, feeling up his sinewy thighs, then his butt. Cody's tool was recharged—he could sense a boundary being tested. Britt was cupping his firm butt in his hands, and then his fingers were dipping into the brush of brown hair running down his crack toward his butthole. Cody had been keeping one eye on the porno for good measure, but then Britt's fingers were definitely massaging his hole, touching it in little jabs that he'd couple with a grunt. When Britt wet a finger in his mouth, it could no longer go ignored.

"Dude, what are you doing?" Cody said.

"Can't help it man, feels too fucking good. You gotta try it."

"No way," Cody said as Britt brought the slick finger to his anus. He pressed it in. "Oh man," he said, looking up at Cody from his contorted position. "It seriously feels amazing."

Cody thought *I'm drunk enough*, and got back down on the floor. He swung his blond-haired legs over his head, parting the thick cheeks of his hairless butt, thrilling to the feel of exposing that most sacred and profane of orifices. He wet his finger just like Britt had done, and brought it to his light-pink hole.

The sensation wasn't entirely new—he'd done it surreptitiously in the shower a couple times—but doing it with Britt was immeasurably different. It was always these moments that were the hottest, when they were doing things they said they'd never do. Britt had an engine grease-stained finger pushed all the way in his butt, then two, and Cody matched him finger for finger and stroke for stroke. Their simultaneous orgasms came like thieves in the night.

50

And so the ass became the focus. They devoted hours to fingering themselves, then sticking anything up their butts that they could find. Sharpie markers, screwdriver handles, an empty tequila bottle. To grease up they used a bottle of Lubriderm Cody purchased for $4.99 at Groom Pharmacy down the street.

A week later Cody, risking ridicule, bought a butt plug from the highway porno store.

"What the fuck is this?" Britt said, turning it around in his hand. Cody explained it, and then they tested it out on Britt, whose enthusiasm swelled along with his cock.

"It just sticks in there, huh?" Britt said, reaching back to feel it.

One afternoon during a break between classes he took Cody out in the woods beside the shop. Yanking down his coveralls, he showed him the red disc of the plug handle pressed up against his butt. He'd kept it in all day. They traded off, then, Britt chancing a few pumps of the plug into Cody's ass before they went back to class.

Later Britt came home with a double-ended dildo, a gesture so enormously suggestive (the thing was shaped like a giant mutant veined cock) he was compelled to say, "Don't tell anybody about this." As if, as if.

Cody had more difficulty stuffing it inside himself than Britt did (all in all Britt had seemed more adept at taking things up his ass, though both pretended not to notice this). But they had many memorable sessions on the couch and on the floor, ass to ass, banging each other in the butt, working in tandem, separate but equal.

The weather started to cool. Cody left town one morning to help his brother move some gravel. When he got back Britt was

gone. Several hours passed and he didn't return.

Cody tried to ignore Britt's absence, but by 5 a.m. it was painful and obvious. He felt weird—he was mad at Britt, but he didn't have a reason to be. He supposed he was worried about him, but that was stupid—Britt could take care of himself.

He lay on his bare mattress in the dark, ringed by dirty clothes, cigarette cellophanes, and empty beer cans. He wondered about this place he was in, the Opera House. Maybe he was lying where the auditorium had been. He imagined a woman on stage, her voice rising to the rafters and filling the space with overbearing sound, the audience taking it in with devouring ears and hungry souls.

Whatever. It was gone now. The lady underneath them was yelling at her kids. The guy next door sold heroin. Anything else was history.

Britt rolled in at noon the next day, Clitter Schreve in tow. Cody desperately wanted to ask what they'd been doing all night, but there was something about the way Clitter looked at him that made Cody go back to his room and shut the door. Britt and Clitter started hanging out a lot, sidestepping Cody like he was a pizza box they were too lazy to take to the dumpster. Cody felt hollow.

One night he made Velveeta Shells & Cheese and offered some to Britt, who ate sullenly at the table. Some wall had been erected between them overnight and out of nowhere Cody could see.

Afterwards Britt had a beer and Cody joined him. They watched TV, talking more as the beer kicked in; then they were swigging whiskey and getting colossally fucked up. Cody was on the floor packing the bong. He dropped some weed and was picking it up when Britt kicked him over.

"Hey!" Cody said, laughing like it was playful. Britt had the ghost of a smile on his face. He kicked him down again. Cody grabbed Britt's leg and pulled him off the couch. They wrestled, drunkenly but seriously, knocking into furniture and using all of their muscle to hold each other down. Britt got Cody facedown on the floor and went for his boxers, tearing them off to expose his bare butt.

Cody felt violated. He grabbed Britt's thigh, then his waist, and flipped him over so hard he knocked the wind out of him. He pinned Britt's hands and yanked his sweatpants down. Britt's hard dick slapped against his stomach. Cody stared at it. He looked to Britt who had his head turned to the side. After a moment he reached out to stroke it, like they used to do. Britt endured a minute of this, then flipped on to his stomach.

Cody was confused, but he put a hand on Britt's ass and Britt backed up to meet it, so he kept it there. He got one dry finger inside him, and Britt was still gyrating his hips, face to the floor, silent. Cody stretched out on top of him, humping his dick against Britt's fuzzy crack, the head of it catching on his hole. Then Britt was adjusting his ass, and the head of Cody's cock went into Britt's asshole, and Britt backed up to take more, the pain of being fucked dry somehow bearable for him. Maybe even necessary.

Cody barely remembered cumming inside of Britt, but afterwards he saw that Britt had cum too, seemingly without touching himself—there was a wet stain on the carpet, like a bad dog's mess.

Cody rolled off and lay on his back. He was beginning to drift off when a red bomb exploded in his face.

He opened his eyes to see Britt's fist coming at him again. Britt, who'd awoken tangled in Cody's limbs only to stumble to the kitchen and finish off the bottle of whiskey, crunched him square on the nose. Hot blood poured into Cody's mouth. He got his bearings and pushed at Britt, who toppled easily. Cody stood up, blood dripping on his socks, on Britt, who was rolling

54

on the floor like some useless thing, waiting for Cody to kick him, punch him, fuck him—wasn't it all the same?

Cody staunched the flow of blood from his nose, wiped himself up with a T-shirt, threw a different T-shirt on his bare chest, and left.

The streets were dark, the lights on Market Street blinking yellow. He wandered, addled, until the sky started to brighten. He found himself in front of the queers' house on Spring Street. Like all the other houses it was dark and quiet. He stepped into their yard and crept through the wet grass along the side of the house. He looked into a window.

He hadn't expected to find them awake, but they were. One man was standing and one was sitting at the kitchen table. Cody had enough time to see that one of them, the smaller one, was pouring two cups of coffee, had enough time to think that they may as well be from another planet before the two men met his eyes.

Dom seemed half asleep. He rubbed his hands over his close-shorn, sandy-haired head, then shuffled to the kitchen and poured a glass of milk. He sat down on the couch next to Randy.

"What are you doing up?" Randy asked.

"Just jittery I guess. What about you?"

"Too much coffee at the rehearsal dinner. Well, that and I'm nervous too. First family gathering since...well...you know." Dom's head snapped to the TV. He took a too-quick drink of his milk and it spilled down the sides of his mouth.

"Crap," he said and lifted his shirt to wipe his face. Randy couldn't help but look. Dom's stomach was thick but tight, with a blondish happy trail that disappeared into his pajama pants.

"I guess it's normal to be nervous," Randy said, shifting his gaze. "Anyway I'm sure Becky would understand if you changed your mind." Dom smiled. He took another swig from the glass, this one more successful.

"I just wish it was over," Dom said. Randy gave him a sympathetic smile. After a moment, Dom lifted his shirt again. He wiped his mouth even though there wasn't anything there, and he did it slowly. He watched Randy watch his body as he tugged his shirt back down, until their eyes met and they realized they'd caught each other in the act.

So Becky got hitched and Randy got drunk. The new couple bought a house in Groom just a few blocks from the Perletti house. Dom, who had a bachelor's degree in communications, took a job managing the Groom Motor Lodge on the highway while Becky looked for work.

One night after dinner Randy fell asleep in the easy chair while Dom watched TV from the couch. The first thing Randy noticed when he awoke was Dom watching him. Dom quickly averted his eyes back to the TV, his face flushing. It took a moment before Randy realized what Dom had been staring at—there was a conspicuous tent in his sweatpants from the industrial-sized boner he'd sprung in his sleep.

The next Friday Becky recruited her brother to help paint

her and Dom's bedroom. When he arrived Dom was already rolling paint onto the walls, and Becky was getting dressed for a job interview in Torrance.

"They called me at the last minute," she said. "Hopefully you guys will be alright?"

"I'm sure we can manage," Randy said. Becky looked to her husband.

"Dom? You'll be okay with just Randy here?"

"Why wouldn't we be?" Randy said again. Becky ignored him.

"Sure, honey," Dom said, and Becky said she'd be back in a few hours.

There was some brief awkwardness after she left, but small talk was one of Randy's strengths, and he easily maneuvered them into friendly waters.

"Is married life all it's cracked up to be?" he asked as he loaded up his brush with periwinkle paint.

"I wasn't expecting anything, I don't think," Dom said. "It's nice though. You know—comfortable. I don't have to wonder about, like, going out on a Friday night, looking for whatever, getting drunk. That gets old."

"You don't like to drink?" Randy said.

"Well, sometimes I do."

"Good, cause I brought a six pack. We can split it." By the time they finished painting they had two beers left. They were cleaning off their brushes and rollers in the utility room, the close quarters heady with the smell of their sweaty bodies.

"Wish the pool was still open," Dom said.

"We should go up to Bolivar Falls," Randy said. "You ever been?"

"No," Dom said, then hesitated. Into the vacuum of his silence rushed sexual tension. Randy hadn't intended it, but there it was.

"I've heard of it," Dom continued, whacking a brush off the side of the sink. "We could take the rest of the beer."

"Sure," Randy said, his heart picking up speed. "Becky won't

59

care, right? We can leave her a note or something."

"Don't bother," Dom said.

After a ten-minute drive they started the two-mile hike into the woods. They were soaked in sweat again by the time they got to the falls, a forest glen with a creek that dropped off into a deep pool. There was graffiti on the rocks and some strewn-about trash, but it had a secretive charm.

"I guess we can go in in our underwear?" Randy said.

"Sure," Dom said, emboldened by the beer and the beauty of the place. He stripped down and Randy followed suit. Dom's tighty-whities hugged the generous curves of his muscular butt and acted like a sling for his beefy cock. Randy was embarrassed to reveal his patterned bikini briefs—a purchase he'd made out of boredom and horniness one night while stuck at the mall with his mom.

Dom swept his eyes up and down Randy's body and Randy did the same to Dom. Before either could register anything Dom turned and ran for the ledge, springing himself over the waterfall and into the air, crashing into the pool below.

"It's freezing!" he called. Randy approached the edge. He felt the slick rock beneath his feet. He jumped, fear and release rushing through his body for a drawn-out instant before he plunged into the water.

"It feels fucking amazing!" Randy said, his breathing short and shallow. They laughed with exhilaration.

Later they lay on the warm rock above the waterfall.

"Did you have a good time at the wedding?" Dom asked.

"Yeah, man."

"It wasn't awkward for you? I mean, you said you thought it might be."

"Well, the open bar helped." Dom laughed. "I don't care what people think of me, anyway," Randy said. Dom drank the last of his beer.

"You mean the fact that you're..."

"Gay. Yeah. That."

"Yeah," Dom said. Birds squawked in the trees. "I was

wondering... Like, how did you know you were? I mean, did you ever date girls?"

"Yeah I dated girls. I even had sex with a few of them."

"Really?"

"Yeah. But I always did stuff with my friends, too. And eventually I realized that stuff was more interesting."

"You messed around with your friends?" Dom said.

"Yeah."

"Like what kind of stuff?"

"Like, you know. Kissing. More than kissing," Randy said. Dom brought the beer bottle to his lips, tipped it back even though it was empty. Randy took a deep breath. "Did you ever do stuff like that? Like before you met Becky?"

"No," Dom said. He turned his head to Randy and smiled. "Not even kissing."

"Kissing's easy," Randy said. "You know—noncommittal."

Dom laughed. "I'd try that. Kissing a guy."

"It's not much different from kissing a girl," Randy said, nervously plugging his thumb into the mouth of his beer bottle.

Dom stood up. He tossed his empty bottle into the weeds and turned toward Randy. His half-hard cock tented his transparent briefs. Randy set down his bottle and stood up next to him, his hefty dick also visibly at half-mast.

"You want to?" Dom said.

"Kiss?" Randy said.

"Yeah," Dom said. They moved toward each other, their cocks hardening. When they came together an involuntary force took over. Their mouths locked and their tongues dueled, desire passing between them thick and hot as molten rock. Randy moved his hands to Dom's back. Dom placed his hands on the smooth sides of Randy's torso. Making out with Dom felt natural and breathtaking, but it was just too much. Randy had to break away.

"Thanks," Dom said, looking at the ground, and the word was a hollow thud. They dressed and headed to the car. The world, having disappeared for a moment, rushed back like a tsunami. They rode home in silence, each mile getting them closer to the lives they'd upended.

※

The strange thing was that after that day, hard as they tried to avoid each other, Becky seemed to do all she could to bring them together. She went whole hog in enlisting Randy's help with their house, making dates that Randy always managed to blow off.

"I saw they just opened a record store on Main Street," she said one night over dinner at the Perletti's. "You and Dom both like music—you guys should go down there together!"

"Sure," Randy said, and Dom nodded politely, while Becky eyed them like they were lab rats.

"Do you like Dom?" Becky asked her brother one night after dinner. Randy was washing dishes while Becky sat at the kitchen table. Dom had already gone home.

"Of course," Randy said. "Dom's a good guy."

"I think he's about the best-looking guy I've ever seen," Becky said. "Don't you think he's good looking?"

"Yeah, he is," Randy said. "He's got a handsome face."

"Are you happy for me?"

"Of course I am. I'm happy for all of us, cause if you hadn't gotten laid soon you would've drove us all nuts."

"Hush up," Becky said. "I hate it when you talk like that." She dipped her finger into a candle, coating the tip with hot wax. "I never thought a guy like Dom would *look* at me, let alone *marry* me."

"Don't say that," Randy said.

Becky shrugged. "I know I'm not the cutest button in the box. But there was Dom, sitting across from me in my Shakespeare class, and he just...I don't know...*listened* to me. Made me feel like I was worth his time. I asked him to go out, and he did. I'd never asked a guy out before. Can you believe that?" Randy toweled off a plate and stacked it with a clink.

"I can," he said, turning toward his sister. "You don't give yourself enough credit, Becky. You've always been shy, but you're great. People just don't get to see it." Becky smiled and cast her eyes downward. Randy went to bed that night with a heavy heart.

On Labor Day Becky arranged a picnic at their parents' house. Dom wore a pair of thin khaki shorts that made his ass look like wrapped cantaloupes. In the chaos of aunts and uncles and cousins Randy lost track of his brother-in-law. He had to piss, so he entered the quiet house and went up the stairs to the bathroom. The door was closed and the shower was running. He figured it was his dad, so he walked in and shut the door behind him.

"I gotta pee," he said after he'd already unzipped. He heard the shower turn off. "Just gimme one second." The curtain pulled back and Randy turned his head. There was Dom, naked, wet, and already half-hard.

"Shit," Randy said. "Sorry." Dom, who'd needed to clean up after knocking whiffleballs around with the kids in the ninety-degree heat, locked eyes with Randy. He didn't move a muscle except for his cock, which arose slowly until it was standing straight up.

Randy could've left the room. It was probably the right thing to do. But instead he stepped forward and wrapped his hand around Dom's fat cock. He raised his face to meet Dom's mouth. As they made out their hands moved like wildfire, Dom ripping off Randy's clothes, Randy feeling every inch of Dom's body. Randy knelt down, his shorts around his thighs and his hard cock jutting out. He took Dom's cock in his mouth.

Dom's lungs deflated. A few passes of Randy's mouth and throat around his cock and Dom was almost juicing. Randy licked his way up his brother-in-law's body, munched on his pecs and nipples, then trailed his tongue down Dom's thigh. He flipped him around. Dom braced himself against the shower wall. Dom's ass was a gift, big and perfect, and Randy dove in. His pink, deep asshole seemed to invite Randy to dig deeper with his tongue. Dom whimpered and pushed back harder.

Randy stood and dropped his shorts so that his buckle clanged against the floor. He grabbed a bottle of shampoo and lubed himself up. He pressed his cock to Dom's asshole and in moments he slid inside. Dom stifled a cry but didn't protest as Randy porked him balls-deep. A minute or so of thrusting and Randy was blasting inside Dom's virgin butt and Dom was spraying the shower wall.

They didn't talk as Randy slid out, pulled on his pants, and left. He went to his bedroom and locked the door; caught his breath. When he came back out Dom was with the rest of the family on the patio, freshly showered and freshly fucked. He had a noticeable glow, and even nodded to acknowledge Randy's entrance.

"It was like you tripped a switch in me," Dom would say years later about that afternoon. "I instantly knew how sex was supposed to feel. I felt so relieved." Randy had apparently fucked the fear right out of Dom, and Dom got bold. Two days later he came knocking on Randy's bedroom door. Randy tossed his liquid-crinkled issue of *Mandate* on the floor, zipped up, and answered the door.

"What are you doing here?" Randy said, ushering a wild-eyed Dom inside.

"I told Becky I was borrowing a record," he whispered. Dom impulsively leaned forward kissed him, knocking their mouths together so hard it hurt. "Here," he said, and handed Randy a key. The plastic, diamond-shaped key ring had the number *28* imprinted on both sides. "I got this room for tonight."

"For us?" Randy said.

"You don't want to come," Dom said, his face falling.

"No, no, of course I do, it's just...Jesus. Okay. When?"

"After two. I'm supposed to be doing paperwork in the back office but the night clerk won't notice." Randy took the key. Dom made it halfway down the hall before Randy thought to call him back. He grabbed the first record off his stack and shoved it in Dom's hands. Dom looked at it: Abba, *Arrival*.

"I already have this one," he said.

Sex at the hotel that night was less furtive than before but even more frenzied. Randy dropped three loads into his brother-in-law in less than two hours—one down his gullet and two in his increasingly insatiable butt.

"I love your dick in me," Dom admitted as they lay beside each other watching the blank TV, the Zen-like hum of the motel room thrumming through them. Then, "Becky wants a baby."

"I'm supposed to be saving money to move to the city," Randy said.

"You're moving?"

"That was the plan. I don't know what the fuck I'm going to do now."

"Me neither," Dom said. They fucked again.

For two more weeks they met at the motel, until Randy couldn't take it anymore and put all he'd saved on a security deposit for an apartment in Pittsburgh. He moved in the middle of the night, telling no one until he called his parents the next day.

That October, Randy heard from his mom that Dom was leaving his sister. No particulars were offered. Randy sensed his mom knew—or at least suspected—more than she was letting on, but he didn't press the issue.

He lay low all winter. He hadn't spoken to Dom since he'd left, though on several occasions he'd driven all the way back to Groom just to see if Dom's car was still parked outside the motel, which it always was.

That spring Randy came home to visit. The divorce had gone through. Becky was even dating a guy named Hugo that she worked with at the state mental hospital in Torrance.

"He likes bird watching," Randy's mother reported. Randy was weeding her garden. "That's what they do together in their free time, watch birds."

"He sounds nice," Randy said. He'd tried to call his sister the week previous and she'd hung up on him.

"Your Aunt Mary called. She wants the whole family up for the Fourth of July. A reunion, she says. It's a ridiculous idea but you know how she gets."

"Hmm," Randy said, yanking plants.

"Did I ever tell you that your father used to date your Aunt Mary when they were in high school?"

"Huh? No," Randy said.

"They were in love—so *she* said. I suppose she must have felt they were..."

"Her and Dad? How long did they date?"

"Oh, a few years I think. Even after high school. In fact they talked about getting married at one point."

"You're kidding," Randy said, sitting up to look at his mother, who was gazing into the distance.

"Even today I catch her looking at him. Maybe I just think I do. Who knows?" She shrugged. "Love doesn't care about anything but itself," she said and walked away, leaving Randy with a head full of questions and his knees in the dirt.

8. Paperboys

They met on an early summer morning with mist over the grass. Carl had been delivering newspapers since March; it was Nick's second day. Their routes intersected on Walnut Street. They found they lived just across the railroad tracks from one another, and like the random combination of a lock their friendship tumbled into place.

Sometimes the papers arrived late at the newsstand. They sat waiting in the back of the store, their newsprint-grayed paperbags protecting their butts from the dusty linoleum. Carl got up and walked past the magazines (the pornos on the top rack tantalizingly wrapped in plastic) to the paperback racks. He leafed through a romance novel, stopped when he hit on a good part, and waited for Nick to investigate.

"What are you reading that for?" Nick asked, and Carl showed him. It was less than three pages of heaving breasts and throbbing manhoods and red-hot centers, but it was enough. Better yet the romance rack was full of them, all creased to the sweet spots for easy access. They would read next to each other in silent appreciation, crouched on the floor below the view of the clerk, knees sore, secret boners folded into their shorts.

"These make me want to play with myself," Nick said.

"Gross," Carl said.

"It's not gross. Everybody does it. Even my dad plays with himself."

Nick's dad Mario collected comics. So did Nick. Carl read them but wasn't into superhero stuff like Nick and his dad. He liked weirder ones, like *Tales from the Crypt* and *The Sandman*.

Mario's den was right below Nick's bedroom. It smelled like wood and rare books and was strictly off limits.

"He has *Playboy*s down there somewhere but I've never

been able to find them," Nick said. He pointed to a vent in his floor. "He can hear everything that goes on up here."

They were having a sleepover in Nick's bedroom, and apropos of nothing Nick decided to change his underwear.

"Don't turn around," Nick said, standing behind Carl. Carl stayed still as Nick's cotton briefs laved down his smooth thighs. "Don't look, I'm naked," Nick said, then a slow sliding up, the snap of fresh elastic. "Okay you can look." Nick smiled a dimpled smile.

"Should I sleep on the floor?" Carl said.

"No, we can both use my bed; we'll just stay in our sleeping bags." When Carl came back from the bathroom Nick was already tucked in.

"Why are you wearing all that?" Nick said.

"I don't know."

"I just wear my underwear to bed. Sometimes I even sleep naked." Nick didn't let go of the issue. "Don't you get hot? That's stupid to wear all those clothes." Carl conceded, but waited till he was under the covers to strip down.

Nick was the first one up that morning.

"I've got a boner," he said.

"You're sick," Carl said.

"It's right here under my sleeping bag."

"At least you have underwear on."

"I don't anymore. I always take them off in my sleep. See?" Nick pulled his briefs from under his body. He tossed them onto Carl's face. They were warm. Carl threw them to the floor, acted disgusted. "So yeah," Nick said. "I'm totally naked with a boner right now."

"What is wrong with you?"

"Nothing. I get a boner every morning, don't you?"

"Sometimes."

"What about right now?"

"No," Carl lied.

"Now I'm touching mine," Nick said, his hand rustling in the right spot.

"Oh my God."

"I dare you to touch yours then lick your hand."

"Seriously?"

"That's not so gross, right? Brandon was daring everyone to do it after gym last year. They all acted like it was sick but I couldn't figure out what the big deal was." Then: "I'll do it if you do it." Carl followed Nick, sliding his hand under his briefs and laying his cool palm on his warm erection. Nick pulled out his hand, slathering his tongue across his palm and fingers without hesitation. Carl followed suit. It tasted salty but not like anything.

"Now put your hand back on it," Nick said. They did, lying with breathless silence, their slick palms against their hard-ons. "C'mon, you've got a boner too. Just admit it."

Just then Nick's dad opened the door. Carl moved his hand off of his crotch too quickly.

"I *thought* I heard that you guys were awake," Mario said, looking into Carl's reddened face.

Nick was a grade behind Carl, but they were both in the same building, Groom Junior High. Though best friends they were removed from one another during school, and their interaction was limited to exchanging hellos in the hall.

In the afternoon they'd walk home together with two neighborhood girls, and it was through those girls that Carl learned Nick was declared to have the best butt in his class.

He couldn't argue with that. Nick's butt was round and plump and he loved to show it off, mooning Carl whenever he got the chance. Returning from their routes, Nick would jump ahead of him in the alley, lowering his shorts over his substantial behind, strutting for Carl's embarrassed amusement.

The two friends had never seen one another's dicks, but once Carl spotted Nick's balls under his boxer shorts, resting against his thigh, and was bold enough to point it out.

"I don't care," Nick said. He looked down at himself, then raised the leg of his boxers until his whole smooth nutsac was exposed. Carl feigned disgust but Nick wasn't moved.

"You're so weird about your body," he said to Carl, which hurt, but Nick couldn't know that the risks weren't the same for both of them, the playing field not level. Carl barely realized it himself.

They played at flirtation. Nick put on Depeche Mode one night, slipping his ass out of his shorts and bumping around his room. Carl sat below him on the beanbag chair.

"What are you doing?" Carl said.

"I'm stripping for you," Nick said in faux-seduction mode. Carl laughed incredulously as Nick lifted off his shirt and wiggled his bare ass from side to side. He got more and more explicit, carefully holding his shorts above his crotch as he pushed his butt back toward Carl's face. He planted his feet wide and bent over all the way, then pulled his cheeks apart. There was his hole, the first one Carl had ever seen, a pink-purplish shock. Nick laughed at his own brazenness, but Carl kept his cool. Taking it further, Nick lay down on the floor, ass in the air, and humped away. He brought his butt closer to Carl's face, and finally got on all fours and spread it wide.

The shock had worn off and Carl found himself with a hard-on, mesmerized at the sight of that hidden forbidden place. He thought of holding out his finger and giving Nick a shock of his own when he backed up his ass, wondering what it would feel like to touch it. He'd touched his own before.

Nick rolled on his back. The song was nearing its end. He threw his shorts-bound legs over his head and as the song died down he flexed his asshole to the beat. It was ridiculous, beyond transgressive, and they both laughed hysterically as Nick dropped his legs and pulled up his shorts. The pup-tent in the front didn't go unnoticed by Carl, but Nick tried to hide it, launching himself belly-first onto the bed.

"That was so gay," Nick said.

⁂

They went to the Groom Senior High homecoming game and walked home together when it got boring. The announcer's voice echoed from the field across the brisk night sky, the field lights on the hill visible as they headed along the road into town.

"You know Chad McCrae?" Nick said.

"Yeah." Chad was a junior like Carl and Nick's older brothers.

"He's going out with Hillary Nagelson. My brother's friends were over last night and they were saying that Hillary ate out his ass."

"Ate out his ass?"

"Yeah," Nick said. "It's like the other kind of eating out, except she did it to his...butthole," Nick said.

"Gross," Carl said.

"She's a slut," Nick said. "I can't imagine how you would do something like that. Unless he'd washed his butthole really good."

"Even then."

"Yeah, it's disgusting either way, but maybe not as bad if he was really clean."

"*Maybe*," Carl said.

Later they were in Nick's bedroom. Nick's parents and brother were still at the game, they had the whole house to themselves. They played Risk and Nick won, as usual. They got bored.

"I wish you weren't here so I could jerk off," Nick said. "Don't act like you don't do it. We both do. Why don't we just admit it to each other? Why is it this big secret?"

"I'll go downstairs if you want to jerk off," Carl said.

"No way. I need to go downstairs too. I get naked and run all around the house when I jerk off."

"You're full of it," Carl said. Nick got on his stomach and started humping the bed. He took down his underwear and exposed his ass, backing it up to reveal his hole.

"Then you pretend you're Hillary Nagelson and I'm Chad," Nick said.

"You gotta get it clean first," Carl said.

"Okay," Nick said, and got up and left the room. Carl was sitting on the beanbag chair, looking at the comic in his hand but not comprehending a frame of it. He could hear running water in the bathroom, though it could have been Nick tricking him. When Nick came back to the room he had just his underwear on.

"I'm ready for you, Hillary," he said and flopped on to the bed with his legs dangling over. He shoved his briefs down around his thighs and took them completely off.

"Oh, *Chad*," Carl said with soap-opera passion, getting between Nick's legs. He took hold of his calves. "Give me that ass, baby." Nick chuckled and raised his butt back toward Carl's face, letting his cheeks spread apart. Nick's sac was drawn up tight below his asshole, the space between them was domed and swollen. Carl moved his hands up higher, let his fingers flirt with Nick's buttcheeks.

"Do it Hillary," Nick kept saying. "Eat my ass." To Carl, the idea was starting to seem less crazy than it had a few hours ago. Nick's asshole was familiar to him now, smooth and pink with downy hair around the rim. There was the distinct smell of Dial soap coming from it, suggesting that he had in fact washed. Underneath that was a musky, familiar smell. He let his face graze Nick's smooth cheeks.

"I can't wait to taste your ass, baby," he said, moaning. Nick backed up abruptly and his asshole made contact with Carl's nose.

"Oh shit," Nick said. He lay flat and looked back at Carl. "Sorry."

"It's what I wanted, Chad," Carl said, and Nick backed up again, but Carl couldn't think of anything else to do. So he just sat back in the beanbag chair. Nick put his underwear back on carefully and remained on his stomach for a good ten minutes. Carl's boner was tucked underneath his waistband. His nose seemed to burn from the contact with Nick's asshole.

He left after Nick's family returned, and when he jerked off that night he tried to time it, so that they would be doing it at the same time.

Mario was supposed to drive them to the comic book store one day but plans changed at the last minute. So Nick and Carl went walking along the tracks. They then veered off into a clearing in the woods. They were farther away from home than they should have been, but they knew the tracks were behind them as they continued deeper in.

At first the sun strobed through the trees but as they went farther the sunlight got watery and weak.

Carl was getting ready to ask Nick whether they should turn around when they saw the shack. It was small, a lean-to, wooden and decrepit, and it sat in the middle of the forest as if it had grown there. There was a door in the front and it was cracked open. Nick crept toward it.

"What if there's somebody in there?" Carl whispered. Nick got closer. He pushed the door and it creaked as it swung in. Carl saw only a pool of dark beyond the frame. Nick peeked inside and motioned for Carl to join him. Carl did, hearing every stick and leaf crunch under his feet.

On the floor of the shack was a gray mattress, half-folded against one wall and littered with dead leaves. On top of it was a billiard cue.

"Holy shit," Nick said as he stepped inside. "Look." He pointed to one corner. Stacked there were porno magazines, at least twenty of them. Nick picked up a few. "These are weird," he said. They weren't the garishly-colored covers of the newsstand porno magazines, they were dark and murky with foreign titles. The cover creatures were enclosed in latex and masks and gagged with red balls.

"We need to get back," Carl said, but Nick was already rolling up four magazines and trying to stuff them down his pants.

"Help me," Nick said. He handed Carl the roll of magazines and lifted his shirt, holding out the waist of his pants. At the last minute he held out his underwear waistband too. "That should hold them better," he said. Carl looked down. Even in the dim light he could see Nick's cock, soft and nestled in the cup of his briefs. He knew that Nick knew he was looking. He slid in the magazines. Nick lowered his shirt.

"You take some too." Carl stretched out the waistband of his shorts and underwear and the ritual was repeated. Nick took his time, rolling and re-rolling the magazines to make them tighter, and unabashedly looking at Carl's penis. "Let's go," he said once he had them inside.

They stepped outside the shack. The woods were even darker. And just there in front of them was a man. He was lying face down on the ground, and how they'd missed him before was a mystery. He was wearing a white shirt and maybe pants. He was motionless, but that was all they saw because Nick took off running and Carl followed. They ran with a fear greater than any they'd ever known, until they were back on the tracks and back in the light.

"He was dead," Nick said when they'd gotten a comfortable distance away.

"Are you sure?"

"He wasn't moving," Nick said, and that was true, though Carl later seemed to remember an empty bottle lying nearby.

They got back to Nick's house but crept behind the garage to where his dad kept a metal barrel for burning. They put the magazines in the barrel, showered them with lighter fluid, and lit them. As the pages disappeared Nick took his dick out and peed on the fire. Carl took his out too. Their urine hit the flames and evaporated. They burned the pile until there was no trace.

Once home Carl sat on the living room chair and took off his shoes. His dad and sister were in the kitchen carving a pumpkin. On his socks were black burrs from the woods. They were dark and menacing, insect-like, with twin prongs that attached themselves to the fabric. He picked them off one by one.

9. Fuck Stuff

"You ever fuck your mattress?" Abe Meyers asked Clitter Schreve one mid-summer's night. Abe took a showy drag off of his cigarette. The two of them had dropped out of high school together early that spring, and were doing their damndest to appear like adults.

"What do you mean?" Clitter said. He looked up at Abe, whose head was framed by the darkening evening sky beyond Clitter's front porch.

"What you do is stick your cock in a rubber, or just get Vaseline on it and wrap it in Saran Wrap. Then you stick your cock in between the mattress and the bottom part and fuckin hump away. Feels awesome."

Clitter's cock started to get hard. Abe's was already and he wasn't trying to hide it. Clitter didn't know what to say. He looked out at the street where the Grekko kids were playing, a mass of crusty children that seemed to grow a new diaper-wearing toddler with each passing month.

"Didn't you fuck a sheep once?"

"Yeah," Clitter admitted, a grin spreading across his twisted face. Clitter's real name was John. Because of his hatchet face kids started calling him Critter. But he had a hard time pronouncing r's; they got rolled around in his mushy mouth, and when he'd object it came out as "Stop cawwing me Clitter," so that was his name now.

"On Jeremy's farm," Clitter added. Jeremy was his cousin. "He fucked it too."

"You fuckin scummy hick," Abe said. He tossed his cigarette butt onto the sidewalk; adjusted his boner. "Did it feel good?"

"Yeah. Kinda smelled though."

"Sick!" Abe said, both of them breaking down laughing.

"You sure it was a girl sheep?" Clitter shrugged.

"Fucking anything feels good," Abe continued. He spit off the porch and wiped his mouth with his t-shirt.

"Yeah," Clitter said.

"I'd fuck just about anything."

"Yeah."

"Wanna go over to my house then?"

"Huh?"

"Go over to my house and fuck stuff."

❌

Abe lived around the block. In some way he and Clitter were cousins, maybe second cousins, Clitter could never understand how exactly they were related.

Nobody was home at Abe's house. Nobody was ever home. Abe's dad had left years ago, his mom was usually at her boyfriend's. The house was a mess but it was a mess everyone was used to, nobody noticed all the sticky things smashed into the carpet and the rings around the bathroom tub and the toilet that smelled like piss and the clothes and stuffed animals and whatever else that was piled into the halls, layer upon layer of the accumulated detritus of their lives, like the fossilized bits of history that make up the earth's crust.

"Let's see what we got in here," Abe said, opening the fridge. Clitter stood behind him, his boner tenting out the front of his cut-off jean shorts. Abe was as horny a fucker as Clitter had ever known. They'd been jerking off together since they were ten, it seemed like. Abe always would talk him into doing it. They never talked about it, but one time Abe had held his hunting knife to Clitter's neck and made Clitter suck him off. Clitter had avoided him for weeks afterward but Abe seemed as freaked out about as Clitter was, and hadn't tried it again.

77

There was a watermelon in the bottom drawer of the fridge. Abe brought it out. He took his knife and cut a hole in it, then set it on the kitchen table.

"Looks good enough to fuck, don't it?" he said, and dropped his pants and tried sticking in his hard dick but it was too big for the hole he'd made. He carved out some more around the edge of the hole and tried again and it worked. Clitter heard the flesh of the watermelon give way as Abe shoved his dick inside it, moaning as he did so. Pink juice streamed out around the edges of the hole and down his dick shaft, dripping off of his hairy balls. Abe held the melon against the kitchen table and humped away until it was Clitter's turn.

Clitter stuck his dick in the slightly warm place where Abe's cock had just been, but it was really like fucking nothing. Abe's dick was wider than his, and the path he'd cleared made the hole loose around Clitter's dick. Still, there was something undeniably exciting about it, humping the melon while Abe egged him on, saying "Fuck it man; get that shit."

Next Abe dared Clitter to stick his dick in a jar of peanut butter, which he did. That felt even better than the melon, because the peanut butter jar was new and none had been used, which gave it a tight, packed feeling. Abe did the same, even tried to fuck it a little but it just got messy. They opened up the back door and tried to coax the next-door-neighbor's dog to come up the porch and lick off their peanut-butter covered dicks, but she wouldn't come. Then Abe made a dare and they each swiped finger-fulls of peanut butter off each other's boners and ate it. The peanut butter was kind of like lubrication so Clitter got the idea to lay their cocks on the kitchen counter and smash their hands over them, so they humped the counter for a bit. They wiped the rest of the peanut butter off of themselves with a dish towel.

In Abe's little sister's room they took a stuffed giraffe, tore a hole in it, and took turns fucking that, but that was more for laughs than anything, posing while standing up with the stuffed giraffe impaled on their cocks and sticking out in front of their

78

bodies.

They went into Abe's mom's bedroom and humped her satin-cased pillows. Abe wouldn't say it but he liked looking at Clitter's butt when he humped. Clitter had a round white butt and it looked good working all back and forth. And Clitter wouldn't admit it but he was kind of fascinated by Abe's big dick, a good inch longer and thicker than his own. Even the ordeal of sucking him off at knife point had left a somewhat positive impression, if the jack-off sessions he'd had thinking about it, afterwards, were any indication.

They went into Abe's mom's panty drawer and jacked off with her silky g-strings wrapped around their dicks. But Abe was saving the best for last.

They greased up with Abe's mom's Oil of Olay and wrapped their cocks in generic cellophane wrap. Then they had at her mattress.

They fucked side-by-side, each focused on the pleasure they were receiving but also reveling in the shared experience of it, the idea that they were fucking the same thing, or same person if you wanted to push the fantasy to its limits. The mattress was their girl, and this was a bonding experience of sorts. Abe came first and Clitter soon followed. They cleaned up together in the bathroom and then they took their guns out into the woods and shot at birds and squirrels and chipmunks.

10. Family Business

Frank DeVeo had no problem with his sons lounging around the house naked. These were the dog days of July and their air conditioning had bused a week ago, so nudity around the house had become *de rigueur*.

With hard-ons, though—that was a different matter.

Lance and Bobby seemed unashamed, though, and made no move to cover up until they saw their father's face.

"Sorry, Dad," Lance said, grabbing a pillow from the couch and holding it over his crotch. He threw one to Bobby who did the same.

Frank turned back to the kitchen, shaking his head. He grabbed a beer from the fridge, opened it and took a gulp. He wondered if he'd overreacted. He remembered what it was like when he was his sons' age—in fact, in the sexually-arid year since the boys' mother, Debbie, had left the family, he could empathize all to well.

Frank owned his own business, DeVeo Landscaping, and this summer his boys had been working with him more than ever (so much that he was considering renaming it DeVeo and Sons). He'd given them the day off but the work had been more arduous than he'd expected; the extreme heat had exhausted his nerves. He supposed he was more irked by their lassitude than by their hard-ons.

He took another drink of beer. Already he could feel it warming his mind. Setting the bottle on the counter, he stripped off his jeans and shirt. He ran the cold glass bottle down his hard, sweaty chest. Hard-ons. Who cared? It was actually kind of funny once you thought about it.

He returned to the living room, holding his beer at his side. His sons had tossed the pillows aside again and were still boned up. They turned from the TV and looked to their dad. Gauging that he'd relaxed, neither bothered to re-cover themselves.

Frank sat on the couch next to Lance. Bobby, the younger of the two, was spread out on the floor next to his feet.

"What's got you fellas so horned-up, anyway?" Frank asked.

"Just this movie," Lance said. "This one lady has these huge knockers." Frank chuckled. The casual intimacy he'd developed with his sons was one of the pluses that had come from Debbie's departure. "She keeps taking her top off too."

"The plot's ridiculous," Bobby said.

"*The plot's ridiculous*," Lance mocked. "You're such a nerd."

"Cut it out," Frank said. He was protective toward Bobby, whose quiet intelligence was often steamrolled by Lance's loud antics. He looked at Bobby's body, amazed at how much he'd matured in the past year. The landscaping work was making his body muscled and defined.

His hard cock was the real stunner, though. It seemed only yesterday he'd sported a hairless baby dick. Now it was thick-rooted and long, mounted from a dense thatch of pubes. Apparently he'd gotten the DeVeo big-dick gene after all.

So had Lance, but no surprises there. Lance was justly proud of his body and showed it off at every opportunity. Frank took in the perfect v-shape of his torso, a waist you could encircle with two hands. His hard cock, lolling against one golden-haired thigh like the tongue of a lazy dog.

They watched the movie in silence for another half hour. The big-titted actress came and went, but his sons' boners never flagged.

"Damn you kids must be horny. I've never seen such rampant hard-ons in my life," Frank said.

"Speak for yourself, Dad," Lance said. Bobby turned and looked at his father's rod-ridged briefs. "You've got it just as bad as either of us."

Frank smiled, shrugged. "Must be all these teenage hormones in the air."

Bobby went to the kitchen and brought back a beer for his

82

dad. He sat on the couch so that Frank was wedged between his sons.

Now they were watching some beach-y MTV atrocity, all toned and tanned barely-dressed young bodies.

"Jesus, you guys," Frank said, "I guess if you can't beat em..." He stripped off his briefs, letting free his sweaty bone. His sons stared at it brazenly.

"Beat em's about the only thing we *can* do, at this point," Lance said. Frank took a gulp of beer. On some level he'd been expecting this. It wasn't like he hadn't noticed his sons' regular ritual of spending entirely-too-quiet hours together in their locked bedroom.

And the four beers he'd drunk had junked-up the workings of his moral compass.

"That's not entirely true," Frank found himself saying. His boys looked up at him. "I bet I could toss off a load by barely even touching myself."

"Huh?" Bobby said. "What, like, with your mind?"

"Bullshit," Lance said, crossing his arms in front of him.

Frank smiled. He leaned forward and grabbed the fresh bottle of beer that was waiting for him on the coffee table. Cracking it open he took a long chug, then set it between his thighs, the bottle ice-cold on his burning hot skin.

He set his boner so that the head of it rested on the bottle's lip. Grasping the base of the bottle, he rubbed the rim of it up and down his shaft. This was his favorite way to cum, with as little stimulation as possible, and he knew it wouldn't take much to release his—what was it? ...Jesus, yeah, at *least* a five-day load.

He kept at it, relishing the feel of the smooth, narrow glass rim against his randy prick. He'd contract his sphincter and make his boner bounce, sometimes plugging the bottle with his fat cock head. His kids watched, incredulous, and his breathing sped up and his blood pumped faster.

"There's no way," Lance said, but the deal was almost done. Increasingly frantic vibrations were strumming from Frank's cock to his mind, until they reverberated like a scream. He swiped the bottle long from balls to shaft and caught the head in bottle's mouth just in time. The first pulse of his orgasm hit, and a thick stream of sperm splashed and sunk into the half-full pool of beer. Shot after shot it came, the boys' jaws on the floor as their dad orgasmed before their eyes.

"No *way*," Lance said. His throes subsiding, Frank lifted the bottle from his still-dripping cock and held it up to the TV's light for his boys to see. His creamy, viscous load marbled the amber liquid.

"Goddamn that felt good," Frank said, wiping the sweat from his face. Lance took the bottle from him for a closer look.

"Holy crap, Dad," he said, and handed it to Bobby who examined it with wide eyes.

"Your turn next," Frank said to Bobby.

"No way, I want to do it next," Lance said, reaching over to snatch the bottle from his brother. Frank sighed. There was just no controlling the kid when he had his mind set.

"The key is to control it, don't let yourself get carried away," Frank explained as Lance pressed the bottle to his boner. "It's a good thing to learn, cause there's gonna be times in your life when you have to hold back."

Lance got a good rhythm going, but he was humping the bottle more than letting it tease his prick, and his technique only unraveled the more excited he got. Soon his fingers were roaming from the bottle to his shaft, and as his orgasm crested his fingers started working overtime, rubbing against the underside of his prick.

Still, it was quite something to watch his son get off. The sight of his young muscles, straining against his skin as he got more and more ramped up. Even the smell of his musky young body—it was both alien and familiar to Frank, like a part of himself he'd lost years ago.

Lance missed the bottle on his first shot and sent it streaming almost all the way to the coffee table. He still managed to make a substantial deposit into the bottle, which Frank and Bobby took time to examine.

"You show him how it's done, Bob," Frank said, as his youngest son went up to bat. Just as he'd suspected, Bobby managed to do it right, keeping strict contact of the bottle's edge against his fat shaft. With long, slow passes he worked up to it, and only minutes seemed to pass before he was blowing his own load into the family gene pool.

Frank slapped him on the back.

"Good stuff, Bobby," Lance conceded.

"Anybody want a sip of my beer?" Frank joked. His boys laughed. The next morning, however, he noticed the empty bottle on the coffee table. It had been full before he'd gone to bed, and he had a pretty good idea it hadn't been poured down the drain.

The next day was their day off and the heat was impossibly thicker. They did what they could to cope with it, and Frank had just settled in to a tub of cold water when Lance barged in the bathroom.

"Oh, hey Dad," he said. His cock, Frank noticed, was half-hard. "What are you doing?"

"Just trying to cool off. I'm sweating like a whore in church."

"I was gonna do the same thing," Lance said, approaching the edge of the tub.

"Not sure that there's room for two in here," Frank said, sounding more unsure than he'd meant to.

"I guess I could try," Lance said. Frank didn't say anything, so Lance stepped in the tub and rested between his father's hairy legs, his back to his dad.

"It's been a while since I've taken a bath with one of my sons," Frank said, trying to lighten the situation. It certainly didn't feel fatherly. His initially-soft cock was smushed against his son's slick lower back, but soon it was at throbbing attention, and there was no way Lance could've missed it.

Lance pressed down on his father's knees and scootched back, lying fully on Frank's furry body. Frank took a deep breath. He looked down Lance's muscled frame and saw his son's hard cock resting against his hairless abs.

"This is nice. Kinda like when I was a kid. Bobby and I used to take baths with you all the time," Lance said. He picked up his father's hands and brought them around his body. Frank felt up his son's sweat-slick chest. Lance shifted, rubbing his dad's boner against his back. "Geez you're horny," he said.

"You're one to talk," Frank said. He ran his calloused hands down to Lance's stomach and wrapped a fist around his son's cock. Lance arched his hips to meet his stroke. They floated together in the water, Lance's liquid movements stimulating his dad's cock while Frank held his son's body in one hand and his son's throbbing cock in the other. They probably would've taken the act to its logical end if Bobby hadn't shown up outside the door.

Frank noticed him and took his hands away from Lance.

"Hey Bob," he said, trying to banish the guilt from his voice. "We're trying to cool down." Bobby stepped inside the bathroom, looking at them curiously.

"Yeah, you should get in too," Lance said. Bobby looked at the two of them and half-grinned.

"This should be interesting," Bobby said, as he stepped inside the tub. Frank sat up to give him room and Bobby crouched tight at the end of the tub between Lance's legs.

"Ain't we a picture," Frank said, reaching out to massage his sons' shoulders.

"Dad was jerking me off just a minute ago," Lance said.

"I know; I saw," Bobby said.

"It felt good," Lance said.

"Isn't that what you boys do with each other in your room?" Frank said. "Jerk each other off?"

86

"That and some other stuff," Lance said.

"Like what?" Frank, said. He almost choked on his next words: "Blow jobs?"

"Yeah..." Lance said, indicating that bj's weren't the end of the story.

Frank hadn't had any beer that day but he felt intoxicated just the same. It was a fiery mix of apprehension, jealousy, and desire. He'd felt similarly the day before, when they'd jacked off together, but what he *hadn't* felt afterward was guilt. They'd all had fun; where was the harm?

"Pheww," Frank said, running his hands down his face. "*That* I'd like to see."

"We'll show you, Dad," Lance said after a beat. "If you want to see it *that* bad." They hoisted themselves out of the tub, dripping water, their cocks three loaded canons. Frank followed them down the hall, the duck being led by his ducklings, all the way to the boys' darkened bedroom.

The boys sat on the bed and their dad sat across from them in the desk chair. All were quiet for an awkward moment.

"Just do what you normally do," Frank said. "Pretend I'm not even here." His sons looked at each other and grinned. They reached for each other's cocks, then fell into position, side-by-side on the bed with their heads at opposite ends, immediately going for a sixty-nine. They went down on each other in a relaxed, practiced way. They seemed to be pretty adept at making one another feel good. Frank couldn't imagine a more perfect arrangement.

They stopped after a few minutes, looking up to gauge their dad's reaction.

"Lance usually cums first," Bobby said.

"That's not always true," Lance said.

"I said 'usually.'"

"Do you guys cum in each other's mouths?"

"Well...yeah," Bobby said.

"That's sort of the point," Lance added.

"And you swallow and everything?"

87

"Yeah..." Bobby said.

"I'm not judging," Frank said. "I'm just curious."

"Like I said, Lance usually cums first, but it's better when we get it at the same time," Bobby said. They went down on each other again, for longer this time. Bobby was able to take all of Lance's cock down his throat, deep-throating him effortlessly again and again. No wonder Lance usually came first.

Frank's own dick was dripping like a motherfucker, the pre-cum streaming down his shaft and collecting at the base. His boys were really getting into it now, heads bobbing with intensity, the air filling with stuffed-mouth moans.

"Whoa whoa," Lance said, coming off his brother's dick. "I could cum any minute."

"See?" Bobby said. Frank stood up and sat on the edge of the bed.

"Are you guys gonna keep going? I feel like maybe I should try to get in on this myself."

Lance sat up. "Well, we used to take turns on each other instead of sixty-nineing. We could do it like that."

"I mean, are you guys alright with it? You know...sucking your dad's cock." To hear it aloud made it seem so transgressive. But Lance and Bobby just shrugged.

"I think it'd be fun," Bobby said.

"Yeah, we were just talking about it the other night," Lance added. "We didn't know if you'd think we were weird."

"Weird? No. I could never think that about you guys. I love you guys, you know." His sons looked both bashful and proud. "In fact I think a blowjob would feel pretty damn good right now."

Lance went first, lying on his stomach and easing in between his dad's legs. Frank rested back on his hands. He couldn't remember the last time he felt this good. Bobby went next, then they took turns, keeping a tight suction on their dad's cock, worshipping the very thing that had made them. With the two of them on their hands and knees before him, their smooth young butts spread out behind them, it was hard not to get ideas.

They looked at him strangely when he suggested eating their asses.

"You mean you guys have really never done that before?" They shook their heads. "Your mother used to do it to me all the time."

"No way," Lance said.

"She was wilder than you'd think," Frank said, resting on his side, the three of them lazily stroking their dicks to keep them charged. "In fact I've got a strap-on dildo around here somewhere that she used to use on me."

"You used to take it up the ass from her?" Bobby asked.

"Don't tell me you guys haven't tried *that* yet."

"Well..." Lance said.

"Lance never lets me do it to him," Bobby said.

"I don't ever hear you complaining," Lance said. Frank cut them off and had them get on all fours beside each other. He buried his tongue in Lance's butt first, then moved to Bobby's hairless, pink crevice. Their asses were tight and tangy. He reached around to feel their moist cocks, stroking both of them at the same time. Almost in unison they pushed his hands away. Frank chuckled into Lance's ass. *To be young again*, he thought, and *quick on the trigger*.

From what they'd said Frank expected Bobby's ass to be the more accommodating of the two, but the more Frank tongued Lance's ass the more he loosened up. Soon he was pushing his dad's head into his butt, rearing back and straining to take more. Frank obliged and slipped a fat finger past his son's virgin hole. He pumped him a few times, then let Bobby have a go at it. The glee Bobby got from fingering his older brother was obvious, and Frank couldn't resist letting him have his first piece.

He talked them both through it, but Lance was a natural. Frank had learned a term from one of his gay clients, and it seemed to fit Lance: he was a "bossy bottom," with all the requisite demands on Bobby to fuck him harder and deeper. Bobby held on for dear life but it was a lost cause for his first time. He blew it in his brother's butt in three minutes flat.

"Good job," Frank said to the both of them. "You alright?" he said to Lance, who still had his ass in the air.

"I could go for another if you wanna fuck me, Dad," Lance said. Frank wasn't above sloppy seconds and he let himself get into it, giving Lance the pounding of his life.

"Oh my god, Dad, your dick...your dick..." Lance blathered as his dad plugged him, and gave him a sharp slap on the ass for good measure. Bobby watched them, jerking his re-charged tool. Frank was sort of surprised by his own stamina.

"You want some too, Bob?" he asked. Bobby nodded, slack-jawed, and got on his back with his legs in the air. Frank lubed him up and switched sons, but Bobby he fucked slow and steady, with tenderness. Bobby seemed sensitive to every jab, every move. Frank took his time. Lance was fingering his ass, obviously ready for more, but he could wait. Frank had already made his decision.

"I'm gonna cum in you, Bob. Can you cum with me?" Bobby nodded. They looked in each other's eyes. Frank felt Bobby's asshole tighten and spasm around his cock, and then he was losing it too, his load shooting deep into his son's hole. He felt something hot hit his back and realized Lance was cumming too, directing his load all over their sweaty, overworked bodies.

"We should kiss, don't you think?" Frank said after they'd collapsed on their backs in a row. "You guys used to kiss your old man all the time."

Lance smirked. "Maybe we'll get into it a little more, now that we're older," Frank added. Lance went first, as if for a smooch, but their lips stayed together and adjusted until they were parted. Frank nudged his tongue between Lance's lips and he opened wide to take it in. Bobby went next, then the three of them did it together in a messy mass of lips and tongue.

This felt good, Frank thought. There was just no way around it. Say it had been the heat that had brought it on, or their hard-ons, or the lack of ladies in their lives. There were any number of excuses but none of them mattered, because who needed excuses in the presence of such deep and elemental love?

11. Kegger

It was June, the woods were lush, and they had a keg. They'd loaded it in Derrick Thomas' truck and taken it to an old propane well that was tucked into a wooded clearing off Derry Lane. By the time the sun fell behind the trees it seemed the whole high school was there. Summer was upon them and there was a feeling like just about anything could happen.

They drank out of plastic cups and kept one ear out for the cops, who'd busted keggers at the well before. The cops had nothing else to do, and citing a bunch of kids would have been the perfect start to *their* summer.

But the cops didn't show and the keg got low. Drunk teenagers piled into one another's cars for one last back-road joint, maybe heading to the diner for a late-night meal, then crashing at whoever's house was the least treacherous, parent-wise.

Four guys remained to drain the dregs. All of them were on the football team at Groom Senior High. They stood beside the keg, swaying slightly on their feet.

"What happened to Stevie?" Derrick asked. He was of medium height, with messy sandy blond hair he kept tucked under a baseball cap.

"Probably fucking Missy Sparacek," said Toby Feldman. He stood a few heads shorter than the rest of them, but he worked out the most and it showed. "Didn't you see them? He was giving her a tonsillectomy half the night."

"I guess I didn't notice," Derrick said, burping.

"You ain't noticing much, friend," said Craig Thompson, slapping Derrick on the back. Craig was the tallest, and though he was the same age as the rest of his friends, he had a mature look that often got him served, *sans* ID, at the beer emporium outside of town. That was how they'd got the keg.

"I'm noticing what a dick you are," Derrick said. "Fuckin Stevie getting some ass and we're here holdin our dicks. Let's do something. Play a drinking game."

"Like what?" said Dan Frye. He was the soberest of all of them.

"How bout a circle jerk," Craig suggested with a grin.

"Fuck, I think I just about would," Derrick said, stumbling toward the keg and topping off his cup.

"Soggy cookie!" Toby said. "I got an Oatmeal Cream Pie in my glove box."

"Craig just wants to do it so he can show off, plus he knows he'll beat us," slurred Derrick.

"Yeah, ole Tripod," Toby said.

"Havin a big dick don't mean anything. It's who can get off the fastest."

"Yeah, and it's not like there's one winner anyway. Just one loser," Toby said.

"Unless you like eatin cum, then everyone's a winner," Craig added.

"Well shit, I'm fuckin horny enough for anything," Derrick said, pawing at his crotch.

"You guys can't be serious," Dan said.

"Give me one good goddamn reason why not, Frye," Derrick said.

"Cause it's fuckin gay," Dan sneered.

"Not if you don't eat the cookie," Toby said, and they all laughed, all except Dan, who downed the rest of his beer and tossed the plastic cup into the grass.

"Fuck you guys, I'm outta here," Dan said.

"Aw, c'mon dude," Derrick said, "You gotta help us finish this keg."

"I gotta get up early anyway," Dan lied. He got in his SUV and peeled out into the dirt access road.

"No big loss there," Toby said. The other guys silently agreed. Dan Frye was their friend, their teammate, but he always sat a little apart from the group. No real reason—they didn't analyze it—but that was how it was.

The three stood in silence for a moment. Craig whistled the chorus to "I Think We're Alone Now."

"Well, whaddya say, Feldman?" Derrick asked. "You gonna get that Cream Pie?" Toby ran to his car and grabbed it. The boys gathered around him as he unwrapped it. Derrick set an upturned cup on top of the keg, and Toby perched the Pie on top of it.

"So what are the rules, exactly?" Toby said.

"Everyone shoots on the cookie. Last one to shoot eats it," Craig said.

"The whole thing," Derrick added. "No pussying out."

"Fuck," Toby said, considering the possibility. "Alright." They unbuckled their pants and pulled them down. Craig was wearing jeans and no underwear, his cock already stiffening as it hit the night air.

"There it is," Derrick said.

"The legend, the myth," Toby added.

"It's real enough—touch it and see," Craig said, moving toward Derrick, who jumped back and yelled, "Fuck off!" Toby was hard too, Derrick less so. The three of them wrapped their hands around their cocks and started stroking. Toby had a lot of loose skin around his fat little cock, and he worked it easily in his fist. Craig stroked his long shaft in one hand and cupped the apple-sized head of it in his other palm, squeezing it like the bulb on the end of a horn. Derrick had a tight circumcision, and had to use spit.

"Fuck, I wish I had some lotion," Derrick said.

"Excuses, excuses," Toby said, his voice catching. He didn't want to lose, but part of him wondered what it would be like to have to eat the cookie. He'd had the inclination to taste his own cum a few times, but the Cum Paradox always foiled that: once you came, you didn't much feel like eating it anymore.

Craig had sampled his own wares many times and would have gracefully accepted defeat, but this was a competition and he had little doubt that he was going to win. In fact he planned to blow second, after Toby (who looked to be ramping up to a finish), just to show that he could hold off.

"Fuck man, you got a big dick," Derrick said, looking at Craig. This was only the second time Derrick had seen it hard, the first being when they'd done something similar to this on the bus back from an away game. Craig started showing off for him, hoisting it in his palm, tossing it up and slapping it back down. Craig was watching him and thinking that it just wasn't fair, genetics or genes or whatever, when Toby stepped to the center of the circle. His shoulders were hunched forward, mouth agape, and forehead scrunched.

"Goddamn it," Derrick said as Toby crouched low, moaning and pounding his dick. His fast and furious strokes slowed to a rhythmic beat. He pointed the head of his dick at the Cream Pie and with a groan he let loose his first shot. A thick rope, it sailed through the air and slashed across the middle of the Pie. Twice more he shot with diminishing returns, but when he'd finished the Pie had several hearty dollops of cream on top.

"Fuck me," Derrick said dejectedly. He watched Craig caress his hog. The prospect of losing, and what that entailed, began to sink in to Derrick's head. He found himself thinking about a video he'd once seen on the Internet. A slutty girl had been getting pounded at both ends by two guys. Afterwards she'd knelt before them, and the guys had shot what seemed like two gallons of cum streaming and dripping down her face. Just as soon as they'd finished, they'd leaned down and licked her face clean. They'd even wandered on to each other's sides, so it was hard to know whether they'd stuck to their own stuff or had ended up eating each other's.

The scene had sort of disgusted him at the time, but now he realized it had stuck with him, had been lurking in the back of his mind. The context of the scene bisected with the reality he was experiencing just then, and the thought of what he might have to do started turning him on, fiercely.

His cock got fully hard for the first time since they'd started.

He could sense his impending orgasm and he began to grasp for it like a light switch in a dark room, thinking he might win this after all.

Unfortunately Craig had registered the change in his friend and began to step up his own efforts. It didn't take much—he was good at keeping himself on the verge. Without fanfare, he crouched forward and unleashed a hose full of cum on the Pie. Toby, stroking his still-tumescent dick, stared in amazement at the volume of Craig's load. Craig had aimed perfectly, too; he even managed to shake the last drop right in the center. Now the Pie was covered in a pearlescent pool of cum about a quarter-inch thick.

"Fuck," Derrick said, not because he'd been defeated, but because he was ready to blow, too. He knelt forward and aimed. His first shot blasted into the cum pool so forcefully that it made a splash. A couple more spurts followed and his aim remained true. His body racked with pleasure, the throes beginning to subside, he readied himself for the moment of truth.

It was now or never. He picked up the Pie. With his still-dripping cock in hand he took a big, sloppy bite.

Some of his buddies' collected load slid right off the top and over his tongue. He swallowed it down, took another bite of the soggy cookie and swallowed, then popped in the final bit. The creamy center mixed with the creamy coating. It was actually quite flavorsome.

"Whoo-hoo!" Toby cheered. Craig applauded too as Derrick, still chewing, held up his hands in mock triumph.

It was the second week of summer vacation and Craig was hanging out at Toby's. Everyone always ended up there. Toby's parents had let him turn the basement into his own private

teenage paradise. He and Craig sat on a ratty sofa (donated by Toby's grandmother), while the mellow sounds of Pink Floyd seeped through the stereo speakers. He had an ugly orange shag rug, bookshelves, tapestries on the wall, and an old lava lamp.

"I wish we had some beer. Or some weed or something," Toby said, throwing a racquetball against the wall where it made a hollow pop. Craig nodded, though he was pleased enough to be out of his mom's trailer in South Groom. Her boyfriend was a dick and a deadbeat who sat around the trailer all day and got on Craig's case. "What'd you do last night, anyway?" Toby said.

"Went out with Tonia," Craig said.

"That girl from Deep Hollow?"

"That's the one."

"What'd you guys do?"

"Nothing much. Got some pizza and went to her friend's place. Hung out."

"Did you get any?"

"Not last night," Craig said, with a grin.

"Can I ask you a question?" Toby said, passing the racquetball between his hands.

"Sure, buddy."

"Does she suck your cock?"

"Yep," Craig said. "And well."

"Must be hard for her. I mean 'difficult.' What with your size and all."

"She makes do."

"No, but seriously," Toby said. "Do girls have a hard time sucking your dick? I mean, it's so fucking big. Do they get it all? Has anyone ever taken the whole thing?"

"Yeah—Darraugh did."

"Oh man. She has a big mouth, anyway," Toby said. Craig chuckled, shifted in his seat. "So she could take you down to the balls, huh?"

"Yeah. She choked on it, but yeah. Honestly, though, it doesn't matter so much to me if someone can take it all the way. I dig it when they dig it, you know? If they're into it, so am I."

97

"That's cool," Toby said. He realized he was hard. After a minute Craig sank down into his seat and spread out his legs. He wanted Toby to see his swollen bulge, to know that they were on the same page. Toby looked, then looked away.

"All this talk," Craig said, reaching down to cup his bulge.

"I know, I'm getting horny too."

"Wanna jack em?"

"Yeah," Toby said after a minute, as if he'd had to consider. He watched Craig unzip his jeans. Craig never wore underwear. His hard pole lunged out. "Man, it really is something," Toby said, feeling his own clothed boner. "Like a feat of engineering." Craig smiled at his friend, stroked his endowment for Toby to see. "A real two-hander, I bet," Toby said. Craig nodded.

Toby started to think. Then he decided not to. "You think I could feel it?" he said. Craig, nodding his permission, took his hand away and rested it on the back of the sofa.

"Have at it, buddy," he said. Toby started to reach toward it when they heard the window opening behind them. They looked over the back of the couch and saw Derrick's face peeking down at them from the high-set window. Their backs were turned to him, though, and he couldn't have seen what they were doing.

"Sup, buddies," Derrick said. He took his head out of the window and stuck his feet through. Craig tucked his boner into his jeans.

"Guess you'll have to take a rain check," Craig whispered to Toby. Toby nodded, flustered. Derrick landed on the basement floor and came over to them. He looked at Toby's red face.

"What the fuck are you guys up to?"

"Just hangin out," Craig said.

"Yeah?" Derrick said. He caught sight of the bulge in Craig's jeans. "Whatever," he said, and plopped next to Craig on the sofa.

Derrick put the incident out of his mind until later that night. He'd obviously interrupted something. Something sexual? The thought made him weirdly jealous. Why'd they leave him out?

Under this were even more conflicting emotions, left over from the kegger in the woods. He found himself jacking off thinking about it—not the incident specifically, but the idea of what it had been. Actually he fantasized about fucking a girl with Craig and doing what the porn guys had done—covering her face with load and then cleaning it up together.

He didn't feel gay. He pulled out a "Barely Legal" from his stack under the bed. paged through it, and he still got a hard on from looking at shaved pussy. It was true that Derrick had never had a girlfriend, but he'd fucked girls before—two of them. Both were skanks well below him on the scale of attractiveness. He had a problem talking to girls he thought were hot. His brain stalled, and then he'd get mean, teasing them until they got pissed at him and left him alone. He sort of hated girls for that reason, but that didn't mean he didn't want to fuck them. He certainly didn't fantasize about making slow, soulful love to a *dude*.

But the strange truth was that, painful as it was to admit, the circle jerk at the kegger had been the best sexual experience of his life so far. There hadn't been any anxiety to it, or expectation. He didn't have to call them the next day if he didn't want to. It hadn't meant anything.

Except that it sort of had.

So the next day Derrick picked Craig up from his mom's trailer and they went for a cruise in the back cut. Derrick tried to keep himself loose and happy, but his feelings were eating at him. They parked in a field off Falling Run Road and passed Derrick's ceramic bong, which was shaped like the devil, the lit weed glowing in a bowl that stuck out of its grinning mouth.

"So what were you and Toby doing last night?" Derrick finally said.

"Nothing much," Craig said. He slapped a mosquito on his arm.

"It seemed like you guys were doing something when I opened the window," Derrick said, his voice shakier than he would've liked.

"Yeah, I suppose we were. We were gonna jack off."

"Oh," Derrick said. Pause. "Why'd you stop?"

"Dunno. I guess we got caught off guard." Craig looked at his friend. Derrick's whole body was tense. "Didn't mean to put one over on you, buddy," Craig said, resting his hand on Derrick's shoulder. "I'm sorry."

"It's okay," Derrick said, taking a deep breath. "I don't know why I care."

"Probably cause you're just as horny as we are. But I'll jack off anytime, anywhere, with anybody. That's a policy."

"Oh yeah?" Derrick said, cracking a smile.

"Yep," Craig said, smiling with him. "Just instated it right here."

"You're fucking crazy, Thompson," Derrick said.

"So I've been told." He waited a beat. "Want to put it to the test?" he said, already reaching for the fly of his jeans.

"It's nothing new, you know—you not being able to keep your dick in your pants."

"Ha, ha," Craig said sarcastically. He unzipped and hauled out his half-hard monster. "You gonna do it too or what?" Derrick was sort of embarrassed that he was already rock hard, but he brought it out anyway. They sat there, stroking their cocks, illuminated by the dashboard lights, the summer night air weaving through the open windows.

"Too bad we don't have a cookie," Derrick blurted.

"Yeah," Craig said. He considered it for a moment. "Though there are only two of us."

"So?"

"Well, the loser's gonna know he's the loser as soon as they other guy starts to cum. So he might as well just take it from the source."

"Oh shit," Derrick said, throwing his head back with a smile. "You're serious?" Craig shrugged. Derrick found himself

100

dangerously close to losing it. He held his dick still. "So the first one to cum shoots it in the other guy's mouth."

"Sure," Craig said. "If that's how you want to do it. Then he can clean up after himself when he's done."

"Oh my god," Derrick said, laughing and shaking his head. The deal they'd just struck had made him so fucking hard and his heart beat so fast that he felt like he'd come if he moved his hand just the tiniest bit. He took a couple deep breaths and dragged his fingertips lightly over the underside of his cock. Craig, ever the cool customer, kept a steady pace on his hog. The same stroke as at the kegger, Derrick noticed—long, two-handed passes on the shaft coupled with palm-squeezes of the bulbous head.

"Won't be long," Craig said, ramping up his stroking. Derrick still didn't dare fist his prick—he was obviously ready to shoot at the slightest breeze, but neither of them pointed this out. "Think I'm gonna beat you, buddy."

"Shit," Derrick said.

"It's now or never, man," Craig said, hoisting up his hips. Derrick leaned down. Craig beat his dick in long, sweeping strokes. "Take it or leave it. Oh, fuck——"

Derrick positioned his mouth over Craig's cockhead. He smelled the cock, salty and musky. Suddenly a hot blast of cum hit him in the lips and chin. He made a split-second decision and took Craig's cockhead into his mouth, just as another spurt shot out. Derrick swallowed it. His tongue connected with the underside of Craig's prick and he dragged it along as he sucked upward, stopping with his lips just around the dick tip. Craig's next shot coated Derrick's tongue, and he savored it for a second before swallowing. He swept his tongue along the underside of Craig's cockhead, urging out more.

"Oh, fuck, bud," Craig said. More cum. It just kept coming, shot after shot of creamy load that set his senses reeling, to where he didn't even realize he was shooting too, his fingers tweaking the head of his own dick and making it spray like a whale's spout. Still he swallowed, swallowed and swallowed,

101

knowing this was best, getting it hot and fresh from the source, and when Craig was done he even stroked that big dick upward from the stalk to the head, like he was eking the last globs of toothpaste from the tube.

Craig relaxed his hips and Derrick let the dick pop out of his mouth. Derrick wiped his mouth as the two of them looked down at the mess he'd left behind—some of his cum was on the edge of the seat, but the majority had splattered the emergency brake. Rules were rules, so Derrick bent down and licked it up as best he could. He sat up and wiped his mouth again.

Craig, smiling and satisfied, his big dick softening against the leg of his jeans, reached over and patted Derrick's stomach. "Those are my babies in there," he said. Derrick chuckled.

"Poor little guys," Derrick said.

"At least they're someplace warm," Craig said. Derrick drove them back to town.

"See you tomorrow?" Craig said.

"Yeah, man" Derrick said, and that was that.

The light was on in Craig's mom's trailer, meaning the asshole boyfriend was home, so Craig wandered off to his spot under the old railroad bridge near the river. He was happy to find, tucked into the rock he liked to sit on, a plastic bag containing a nearly whole joint of some pretty great stuff that he'd stashed there a week ago. He sat, smoking serenely, listening to the wind in the trees. It took him a minute to realize why he felt so relaxed— he'd gotten off, of course, and in a pretty singular way. One of his best friends had taken his load. It seemed his *other* good friend was after his dick, too. As long as neither of them got too hung up about it, it was looking to be a pretty great summer.

※

Craig met up with Toby at the field the next afternoon,

where a group of kids had gathered to watch the girl's softball team practice.

"Is anything going on?" somebody asked.

"I'm trying to buy some weed but I can't get a hold of my dude Jake," said someone else.

"My brother's back from college, he might get us a case."

And so it went, the futile plans and laments of bored teenagers.

"Where's Derrick?" Toby asked Craig.

"I think he's at his uncle's," Craig said.

"I got like half a joint if you want to go back to my place and smoke it," Toby whispered.

"Right on," Craig said, and they extricated themselves from the group.

"You guys are going to get high, aren't you?" Dan Frye yelled. Toby and Craig shrugged as they walked away. "Fuckin bogarts!" he yelled. Someone told him to shut up.

They headed up the hill to Toby's car, Toby in the lead. Craig watched Toby's fine little ass, which bulged so expressively out of his khaki shorts. He couldn't help himself. He put his hand out and gave it a hearty pinch.

"Hey!" Toby said, laughing as he took off up the hill. Craig charged after him.

"Shake that ass!" he chided as they raced to the car. He caught up with Toby and gave his butt a slap. For a moment Toby let Craig's hand rest there, cupping it.

"What a sweet ass," Craig said.

"You know it, man," Toby said. His ass was pert but substantial, almost defying gravity. It arched out from his lower back with a graceful lilt, like a ski jump. It was almost completely hairless—Toby barely had hair under his arms, even. And from certain sessions with a mirror, Toby could confirm that his asshole was pretty sweet, too—pink and smooth.

Toby had never paid much attention to his ass until he'd gotten with his second girlfriend, Mindy Diesner. With his first girlfriend he'd merely lost his virginity, and the three

103

"Probably."

"I know I could cum looking at your ass," Craig said.

"You really like looking at it, don't you?"

"Yeah I do," Craig said.

"Well, how about this—I'll let you cum looking at it, but then you have to stroke me off." Craig thought for a second.

"Deal, but I want you on all fours."

"Just on the couch right here?"

"Yep." Toby flipped around, his backside to Craig, and assumed the position, spreading his butt wide for Craig's viewing pleasure. Craig reached out to touch it again. His big hand covered almost one whole cheek entirely. He rubbed it, letting a fingertip drag across Toby's hot hole. Toby jerked forward and gasped. After a moment he relaxed and pushed back toward Craig's hand. This time Craig let his finger rest against his asshole.

This was unexpected, Toby had to admit, but it felt damn good. Craig took his finger away and wet it in his mouth. He slapped his fat wet fingertip against Toby's hole again. Toby clenched and relaxed, clenched and relaxed, using one hand to hold himself up and his other to tweak his hard dick.

Craig brought his face closer to Toby's ass. He touched his tongue to the rim of Toby's hole, and Toby moaned. Craig flicked his tongue against it again. Toby bucked forward.

"Holy shit, Thompson, you're gonna make me cum if you do that."

"So, cum."

"But that's not the deal."

"Ain't this even better?"

"So you're gonna tongue my ass until I blow my load?"

"Sure. But then what are you gonna do for me?"

"Well, shit...I'll stroke *you* off, I guess" Toby said.

"Deal," Craig said, holding his hard cock in one hand. "But we have do it at the same time."

"Huh?" Toby said, looking behind himself at Craig.

"Sixty-nine, man," Craig said. He scooted down on the couch

106

and Toby positioned himself over him. With Craig's tongue dragging across his ass crack and Craig's big dick available to him, Toby realized he had the best of both worlds. He'd wanted to stroke Craig's cock, to watch him spurt, ever since they'd been interrupted by Derrick the week previous. It was natural, he told himself, to want to experience a how a dick as massive as Craig's worked.

Craig's tongue in his ass was an added bonus. After Mindy, he wasn't sure if he'd ever find somebody freaky enough to play with his butt again. Craig was a freak of course, everybody knew that, but Toby had never considered the possibility of all-out fooling around with him, until now.

For that matter, Craig was eating him out a sight better than Mindy had, pulling his cheeks apart, tickling his hole with the tip of his tongue before burying it in as far as it could go. Toby worked Craig's towering prick with two hands. It was so close to his face. It wouldn't be the end of the world if he put it in his mouth, he realized, especially in light of what Craig was doing. He popped the head between his lips and sucked down as far as he could. Craig moaned, his tongue still dipped in Toby's butthole. After a while Toby found a rhythm.

Craig wet his finger again and pressed it to Toby's loosened, wet hole. Toby moaned around Craig's cock as Craig slipped his finger inside of him. He let it rest, then pushed it in some more. Toby let Craig's dick slip from his lips with a pop.

"Oh fuck, man, what are you doing to me?"

"It feel good?" Craig said. He pushed in past his second knuckle.

"Oh, Jesus. Yeah. Yeah it feels good."

"Keep sucking my cock," Craig said. With a moan, Toby went back down on him. They continued like this, stopping several times at the edge. Finally Craig slid out from underneath Toby, holding him down in position. He knelt behind Toby and slapped his fat cock against Toby's moist hole.

"Oh man," Toby whimpered. "Don't do that."

"I just want to ride against it," Craig said, trying to maintain his cool. He pushed forward, riding his cock against Toby's crack. After a minute Toby started to push back against it. Craig did it a few more times, until his dick head caught against Toby's relaxed hole. He rested it there, letting it build up pressure. He got some spit on his palm and slicked the end of his dick with it. He pressed it to him again.

Toby held his breath. Craig knew there were limitations to what they were doing—broken-in pussies could barely handle what he had to offer, let alone a virgin ass—but he couldn't resist jabbing a little deeper. He felt Toby stretch more and more with each jab, but Toby never protested, not even when Craig's cock head breached his hole. Toby cried out, full-throated.

"Oh, Jesus," he said in a deep groan. "Fuuuuck...fuuuuuck."

"Hold on buddy, just a minute...I'm gonna shoot."

"Shoot it in me dude, do it...fuck, I'm cumming too." Toby's asshole clenched around Craig's pecker head and that was all it took for Craig. His nuts unloaded into his friend's butt. He held on steadily to Toby's hips as Toby's ass bore down in tight bursts, his own load splurting across the sofa in splattering blasts.

Finally they finished. Their bodies were sheened in sweat. Toby became aware of how different he felt. His ass was warm, glowing, stretched out. He felt relaxed.

Then the phone rang. Once. Twice. Thrice. Upstairs, Toby's mom picked it up.

"Toby!" she called down. "It's for you!"

"Fuck," Toby said, detaching himself from Craig's cock without fanfare and walking over to pick up the phone.

"Who was it?" Craig asked after he'd hung up. He was slipping his jeans back on, and he looked about as relaxed as Toby felt.

"Derrick. He wants us to meet him at the diner."

So they went, after Toby spent some time in the bathroom. Derrick had already got a booth. He knew something was up as soon as Craig and Toby walked in, and despite himself he found that weird jealousy surfacing again.

"How was your uncle's?" Toby asked after they'd seated

themselves across from Derrick.

"Alright. What'd you guys do?"

"We fooled around in Toby's basement," Craig said. The other two looked up at him, startled.

"I don't like secrets," Craig added. He looked at Toby. "In fact me and Derrick messed around in his truck two days ago."

Derrick and Toby exchanged the briefest of glances, then looked back down at their menus.

The waitress came and they ordered. By the time their food arrived the awkwardness had passed, and they were able to sit back and enjoy their meals.

12. The Hippie Down-Low

The three beautiful hippie boys passed Nate on the parkway in their chugging red Honda. He saw them only briefly but the image seared: their easy smiles, the way the late-afternoon sunlight backlit the ropes of smoke from their joint. Their lives seemed effortless and full.

And that was, in fact, the truth of it. The hippie boys had their own jokes, language, and intimate history. It formed an aura that anyone could witness but few could access.

Their Honda told the story under its mats and in the cracks of its seats. Cigarette cellophanes that once held kind buds, sticks from the ends of burnt Nag Champa, a hacky sac someone had lost and forgotten about. It was all there: country cruises in the back cut, late-night beer runs, outdoor summer shows.

Like Nate, the hippie boys were on their way to the Dead show at the Starlight Amphitheater, forty miles outside of Groom. But Nate was driving a year-old Grand Am, and the girl beside him, Jill, was sullen as she packed a bowl of dirt weed. It was her car. The only reason Nate was along was because she'd bought him a ticket. He was sure she had a crush on him, which only made it worse. He would've given anything to be in that golden moment with those boys, but all he could do was watch as they passed.

Jill surprised him at the show with an eighth of shrooms. Later, when the landscape had begun to melt and merge with the sky, Nate realized he'd lost track of her. He hadn't done it on purpose, but he felt carefree for the first time that day.

Galactic was the opening band. Nate was lying on the grass wondering if the stars in the darkening sky were actually there, when someone looked down on him.

"Anything interesting up there?" he asked. He had a wide smile on his handsome, scruffy face.

"Lots," Nate said.

"I'll bet," the guy, whose name was Conrad, said. Nate started to get up, and the guy held out his hand. Nate took it. It was warm. The guy pulled him up, and Nate saw all three of them. It didn't seem possible, yet there they were.

Next to Conrad stood a pale, dreadlocked guy, named Jake, who passed a glass pipe to the third—a short but bearish guy who they called Pounder.

"Are they coming on soon?" Pounder said. He took a hit from the pipe and exhaled, looking at Nate through glassy eyes. "I hope they play 'Saint Stephen.'"

"They might," Jake said. Nate would've been next in line for the bowl but Jake grabbed it from Pounder's hand. "Stubby said they played it in Seattle last week." He brushed back his immaculate white-boy dreadlocks before taking a hit. "'Saint Stephen' into 'Dark Star,'" he said through held breath.

"Oh man, if they play 'Dark Star' I'll suck their dicks," Pounder said.

Conrad laughed. "You'll suck their dicks if they play 'Happy Birthday.'" Conrad took the bowl that Jake held out to him, but passed it to Nate instead. He smiled as Nate held the bowl to his lips. It crackled and glowed.

Conrad introduced him around. Jake shook his hand but didn't smile. Pounder seemed too fucked up to care about anything. Conrad danced next to Nate in the grass for the entire show. Once Nate considered telling him how he'd seen them earlier, how he'd envied their lives and lamented his. Then he inhaled, exhaled, and let it go.

Somehow he was still with them in the parking lot. His trip

was subsiding into an electric buzz.

"Did you come with anyone?" Conrad asked. His arm kept brushing against Nate's.

"Just a girl."

"You should come party with us."

"She was my ride."

"We can be your ride," Conrad said. He was all straight teeth and floppy hair and a sinuous body that flexed under his t-shirt and shorts. "We live just outside of Groom."

"That's where I live."

"No shit?" Pounder said, stumbling beside them, a beer in one thick hand and a packed bowl in the other.

"Don't you have to go to school tomorrow?" Jake said with a sneer.

"I graduated last year," Nate said.

"Yeah, I mean, fuck it," Pounder said. He put bowl to his lips but blew out. Pot flew everywhere.

"Aww fuck man!" Jake said. Conrad shot Nate a grin. They floated through the hiss of nitrous tanks and the murmur of the dispersing crowd. Just before they got in the Honda, Nate caught sight of Conrad cupping Pounder's butt in his hand.

🗿

An hour later they were approaching Conrad and Pounder's house, which looked to be a converted garage. There were no windows. Strange how it sat alone, and only a yard from the roadside. The front door was open and warm light from the room spilled out on to the dark road. Any person in a passing car could glimpse the back of a couch, an orange lamp, a wood-paneled wall covered in posters.

"You guys just leave the door open?" Nate asked as they pulled up.

112

"Trisha does that," Jake said.

"She's hoping some dude'll breeze in off the highway and sweep her off her feet," Pounder said.

"Fuck off," Jake said. The four of them headed inside. Trisha was lying on the couch watching "Cops." Jake kissed her forehead.

"What the fuck took you so long?" she said, and Jake sat next to her to do damage control.

"Dude, he needs to get her the fuck out of here," Pounder said once they were in the kitchen. He grabbed three beers from the fridge.

"Stacy's coming to pick her up after work, just relax," Conrad said. Nate took a drink from the beer. It was ice-cold and hoppy. "So Nate, who was the girl who took you to the show?" Conrad asked.

"Nobody. Just a friend."

"And you left her there?" Pounder said. He held out his beer and Nate clinked it with his. "That's awesome."

From the living room came Trisha's cigarette-roughened voice. "I fucking *told* you I don't care," she said. Jake was muttering: "Baby, baby..."

"Do whatever the fuck you want," she continued. "You will anyway."

"Love," Conrad said.

Once Trisha was gone Jake lightened up considerably, packing copious bowls of some of the best weed Nate had ever smoked. Jake found Nate to be a courteous audience for his opinions on weed—the best strains and effects of various growing conditions and other facts that were meant to impress. Nate was just happy to be on his good side.

There was an undercurrent in the room that Nate couldn't place. It could have been from the mushrooms, but it felt more anxious than that. It felt sexual; not that he was schooled in such matters—Nate was a virgin. Basically.

Junior year he'd let his girlfriend at the time, Alexis, blow him at a keg party on Derry Lane. He'd managed to cum by

113

thinking about Matthew McConaughey. Alexis went off to college in Arizona a month later and he was relieved to have dodged any further bullets.

Now Nate was working at NovaStar, a telephone survey gig in Latrobe, and living with his parents in Groom. He had work friends, including Jill, and they'd spend evenings driving around and getting high. Something was missing. His friends were by default, since everyone else had split. He'd remained, in a netherworld between high school and whatever came next.

"*No more beer*," Pounder said, cutting off Jake's soliloquy on the mechanics of a superior gravity bong. "What are we gonna do now?" Pounder said. He was gnawing on a block of raw ramen.

"Truth or dare?" Conrad said.

"Who goes first?" Pounder said.

"You do cause you asked," Jake said.

"Fuck that—the new guy! You have to pick one—truth or dare?" Pounder slurred.

"Truth I guess."

"You pussy!"

"Shut up Pounder," Conrad said. "Okay, truth...how many times a day do you jerk off?"

"I don't know. Maybe once?"

"You're shittin me," Pounder said.

"I live with my parents..."

"That's no excuse."

"Jake next," Conrad said. "Truth or dare?"

"Truth."

Pounder cut in: "Have you ever fucked Trisha in the ass?"

"You think she'd let me near that?"

"Huge surprise," Conrad said.

"Me next!" Pounder said. "Dare dare dare."

"Okay..." Conrad said, with a glance at Nate. "I dare you to make out with Jake." Pounder shrugged. Jake leaned in. Pounder pulled Jake's head to his and mashed their mouths together. It wasn't silly—there was tongue on both sides. It was a jolt to Nate's whole body—everything changed.

They broke apart. Pounder wiped his mouth. Jake pulled back his dreads and secured them with an elastic band. He looked at Nate and laughed.

"I think we blew his mind."

"Conrad's next."

"Dare," Conrad said.

"Make out with Nate," Pounder said. Nate had known it was coming. Conrad looked at him.

"Shall we?" he said, stepping toward him. Nate leaned forward. It was easy, Nate thought. How could it have been so easy this whole time? Their lips met, then their tongues and there was nothing and everything to it. Conrad's mouth tasted sharp like cigarettes. Their bodies came together. Conrad wrapped his arms around Nate's back, bringing them closer still, and all of it went straight to Nate's dick.

Then it was over. Pounder and Jake were clapping and whistling.

"Look, he's totally hard," Jake said, pointing at the front of Nate's shorts.

"Take it out, man," Pounder said.

"Leave him alone," Conrad said.

"Fuck that, I'll show mine," Pounder said. He yanked down the front of his patched pants, showing his dense auburn pubes and a fat, perky cock that bounced in the air.

"Yeah, but that's not what we wanna see," Jake said, and spun him around. Pounder braced himself against the counter as Jake pulled Pounder's pants down over his ass. It was a big, firm beauty. "Spread it dude—show the new guy." Pounder kicked off his pants and spread his legs. Jake gave the ass a slap. "That's the stuff right there," he said, fondling himself through his gauze pants.

Nate watched in a daze. Of course it had all been leading up to this. Conrad had taken off his shorts and was now stroking a long cock that stood from a thatch of jet-black pubes. Jake was untying his pants.

"Here comes the big reveal," Conrad said. Pounder turned around eagerly. Jake let his pants fall to the floor—he wasn't wearing underwear. Hanging there was the biggest dick Nate could've imagined. It looked like a submarine. The thickness of it tapered at the head, which was uncut and half-sheathed, the head slick and moist. "Something, isn't it?"

"Don't be afraid," Pounder said. He took Nate's hand and brought it to Jake's dick. Nate wrapped his fingers around the thing, which was hot, pulsing, and alive. "Biggest dick in the Livermore valley," Pounder said. Nobody laughed. Nate hefted it in his palm; let it glide back and forth. Jake was smiling down at him. He seemed used to the attention.

"You can try sucking it," Conrad said. Nate looked up. "If you want." Nate paused. It was too much, the three of them looking at him like that.

"Don't mind if I do," Pounder said, taking Jake's cock from him. He dropped to his knees and pointed the cock at his open maw. Holding Jake's balls with his other hand he gobbled down his dick, all the way to the base. Jake's lungs deflated. He took off his shirt. Pounder went for another pass, then another, his tongue curling underneath.

Nate became aware of Conrad moving next to him.

"You *are* hard," he said in his ear, reaching down to feel. "Mind if I take it out?" Nate didn't answer, and Conrad slipped his hand underneath his shorts and around his dick. "Feel mine," he said. Nate reached back and took it in his hand. He turned around and their mouths connected. Conrad dropped Nate's shorts to the floor. They held on to each other's arms and pressed their naked cocks together. Nate could hear Pounder slurping on Jake's cock; Jake's increasingly labored breathing.

When he looked up he saw that Pounder was bent over the counter again, now totally naked. Jake knelt before him, his head buried between the big melon cheeks of Pounder's butt. Pounder groaned low and long.

Jake stood up and drummed his meat against Pounder's ass.

"Who's gonna do the honors?" Jake said.

"He doesn't care," Conrad said, reaching over to caress Pounder's ass cheek. "Slut'll take anything that comes his way." He gave the cheek a slap. Pounder remained prone, his ass presented to them.

"What about this?" Jake said, picking up a beer bottle. He swigged the dregs then got the mouth and neck of the bottle slobbery. He spread one of Pounder's cheeks and brought the bottle to his asshole. "Watch," he said to Nate, and pressed it in. Pounder groaned as the bottle entered him. Jake pushed it as far as it could go. He took his hand away and the bottle stayed. Jake and Conrad chuckled.

"You wanna try it?" Jake said, looking to Nate. Nate kicked off his shorts and went over to Pounder, taking the base of the bottle in his hand. He could feel the tight grip of Pounder's asshole around the bottle's neck as he pulled it out then in. "No need to be gentle," Jake said, taking the bottle from Nate. He jammed it hard and steady; and Pounder only whimpered and backed up for more.

Conrad left and came back with a huge pump-top bottle of lube. He set it on the counter. Jake reached over and squirted some in his palm.

"What are you doing?" Conrad said.

"First dibs, man—you got it last time."

"New guy gets first dibs," Conrad said.

"Whatever," Jake said, grimacing. "Here, let me see your dick." He took hold of Nate's cock with his lubed palm and got it slick. Then he removed the bottle from Pounder's ass and set it on the counter with a clink. He put more lube on Pounder's hole. "He's ready for you dude. Have at it."

"Relax, man. I don't think he's done this before," Conrad said.

"No way," Jake said. Nate blushed.

"Don't worry about it, buddy," Conrad whispered in Nate's ear. "Go as slow or fast as you want—don't sweat it if you pop quick."

"Fuck him, man," Jake said.

"*Somebody* fuck me," Pounder said. Conrad helped get Nate's dick inside. The heat was what struck him—like a rolled-up electric blanket. It was tight, too. He felt like he should hold still and get his bearings, but some instinct took over and he backed out, then shoved it right back in. He was drunk, high and tripping, and Pounder's ass was drawing him in like water down a drain.

Jake had reached underneath Pounder and was whacking him off. "He's gonna shoot already," he said of Nate.

Conrad said in Nate's ear: "Cum inside him, man—lube it up for the next guy."

"I think he's already cumming," Jake said, and it was true. His juice had just spilled out of him, the tenor of the room so pitched that it felt like the continuation of a sustained climax.

He was done so he slid out. Conrad clapped him on the shoulder. Jake took his place and was making a show of slapping his boner against Pounder's sloppy hole.

"Behold the master at work," Conrad said. "At least he'd like to think so." There was no denying that Pounder perked up when he felt Jake's hog at his back door, a fact that made Nate feel slightly inadequate. Pounder spread his cheeks and waited. Finally Jake slid it home.

"*Fuck*," Pounder cried out. Jake fucked showy, running his hands through his dreads, flexing his abs as he swung his hips in slick little thrusts. Nate watched, amazed at the sight of something so large breaching something so small, the rim of Pounder's asshole stretching elastically around Jake's cock.

Jake went on for a good ten minutes before he stepped aside to give Conrad a turn.

"Wish me luck," Conrad said to Nate. Hot as it had been to watch Jake's big dick pierce Pounder's butt, Nate liked watching Conrad the best. Conrad really seemed to enjoy himself, varying his thrusts between quick jabs with the head and long pistons inward. He clutched Pounder's torso as he screwed, sliding his dick all the way out, poising it at the entrance, and driving it back inside. Jake did the duty of jerking Pounder off, the three

119

of them going at it like a well-oiled machine, or maybe just a well-practiced routine.

Conrad was obviously going for the gold. His thrusts got faster and his face flushed red.

"Oh man, he's blowing," Jake said of Pounder. Conrad took hold of Pounder's ass and pounded it savagely. His eyes found Nate's. He was breathing like a locomotive and it was obvious he was cumming. "Yeah man, cream that ass," Jake was saying, but Conrad's eyes never left Nate's, not even after he'd finished, relaxing his body on to Pounder's, catching his breath. He gave Pounder's butt a slap and slid out.

"Thanks for the good time," he said.

"Whenever, chief," Pounder said, turning around. His cock dripped on the linoleum as he walked to the fridge. He chugged a carton of orange juice.

"Guess you're spending the night," Conrad said to Nate.

They said goodnight to the others. Pounder shook his hand and said, "Good job."

"You'll get better," Jake said. Still half-hard, he led Pounder to the couch. Apparently the party wasn't over yet.

Conrad motioned for Nate to follow him. Just before they turned down the hall, Nate looked back to realize the front door was still open. He didn't consider the fact that Jill would be driving by on her way back from the concert, didn't imagine her sadness at being ditched or consider that the glimpse inside the strange open doorway would make her wonder, to yearn for a life she'd never lead.

13. Woods Club

Jeremiah was bored, sitting frog-legged on the curb. He picked at the scabs on his knees. He picked up a rock and scraped it against the sidewalk. It made a jagged white line on the nubby cement. A car drove by and, without thinking, he pulled his arm back and threw the rock at it.

It connected with a tinny *thunk*. The car screeched to a stop and Jeremiah bolted. He heard a man shouting at him but he just kept going, cutting through his grandma's back yard and down the alley then down Lear Hill, the steep road he'd wiped out on the day before, while coasting on his skateboard. His body seemed to career ahead of him, his legs struggled to keep up. The air whipped past his face and got cooler as he descended.

Then he was at the bottom. He propped his hands on his thighs and caught his breath. The guy wasn't coming after him.

The light was dimmer here, the vegetation thick, pungent and cummy. It choked the abandoned houses and empty lots of South Groom, the low end of town.

He cut through a yard and came upon the railroad tracks. Past them was a dirt path that led into the woods. His grandma was cutting hair at the shop in her house, and she'd had at least three white-haired ladies waiting when he'd left. Nobody was going to notice he was gone, so he started down the path.

The trail became overgrown and hard to navigate. He was about to turn around when he noticed the treehouse. It sat in a beechnut tree a few yards away from the trail, a crude platform with rails on the sides. Jeremiah tramped through the high weeds to get to the clearing around the tree. There was a wet pile of clothes just at the edge of the clearing. Rungs were nailed into the trunk, and he was halfway up when he heard people coming.

There were three boys, all around his age, coming down the

path he'd just taken. They caught sight of him in the treehouse and stopped short. He heard them murmuring: *There's someone there.*

"Who goes there?" said the tallest one, a towhead with silvery eyebrows and squinty, reddish eyes. The other two followed him to the base of the tree. Jeremiah hopped to the ground. "What the hell were you doing in our treehouse?"

"Nothing," Jeremiah said.

"These are our woods and our treehouse," the squinty one said.

"Yeah right, like you built it," Jeremiah said.

"You better split if you know what's good for you," he said.

"What are you gonna do?"

"I'll deck you."

"I'd like to see you try."

"What's your name?" asked the shorter boy. He had dark hair that fell over his eyes. He gave Jeremiah a smile that made him look like a fox.

"What's yours?" countered Jeremiah.

"Peter. This is Gary," he said, motioning to the towhead, "and this is PeeVee," he said, motioning to a big lump of a boy with a bowl cut that framed his knobbed forehead.

"You think you could take me, is that it?" Gary said. Jeremiah relaxed a little. Gary wasn't any bigger than him, and he seemed like the only hostile one.

"Yeah, I do. You don't own these woods, anyway. It's public property."

"We have a secret club," Peter said.

"Sounds stupid. Not that I even care," Jeremiah said. He kicked at the tree and dislodged a chunk of bark.

"Do you jerk off?" Gary said. Jeremiah's heart quickened.

"No," he said.

"You don't jerk off?" Peter said. Gary climbed up into the tree, Peter and PeeVee followed. Gary reached into a knot hole and pulled out a stack of magazines. "*Playboys*," he said to Jeremiah with a leer. Jeremiah climbed two rungs to see.

"You can't come up here, it's only for people in the club," Gary said, handing out the magazines. The three of them sat in a circle on the treehouse floor. PeeVee flipped through one and immediately started pawing his crotch, the bottom half of his mouth hanging open.

"Who are you anyway?" Gary said.

"Jeremiah."

"Where are you from?"

"Pittsburgh. I'm staying with my grandma for the summer."

"You can look at one if you join," Gary said.

"How do I join?"

"You have to say you love jerking off," Peter said.

"That's dumb," Jeremiah said.

"Just say it," Gary said.

"Alright: I love jerking off."

"Good, you can come up," Gary said. Jeremiah sat in the circle next to Gary and PeeVee. Gary handed him a magazine. It wasn't the first one Jeremiah had seen—once he and his best friend had snuck into the best friend's brother's room to find his stash, but they hadn't had much time to look at them. He paged through, his head adjusting to the sight of naked bodies. Here was an actress from a TV sitcom, nude and holding a newspaper over her breasts, her pubic hair a black shock against her white thighs.

"Gimme that one," Gary said to PeeVee, and snatched a magazine out of PeeVee's hands. PeeVee sat dumbly until Gary handed him a different one.

"What's wrong with him?" Jeremiah asked.

"He's retarded," Gary said. He reached over and slapped PeeVee in the face. The boy flinched but he didn't move. "He lets you do anything," Gary said.

They passed the magazines around. Most of them had lost their covers, the pages were loose on the staples.

"Getting boned?" Gary asked. He spread his legs and motioned to his tented crotch. "Look," he said. Peter laughed. "Now you."

123

"What?"

"Show your bone."

"No."

"You have to if you want to be in."

"I thought I was in already."

"That's just the first part. Now we have to see how big your boner is."

"If it's too small you can't join," Peter said. Jeremiah looked at Peter and his icky grin. He realized a profound dislike for the boy which he couldn't quite place.

"Can you even shoot yet?" Gary asked.

"Yeah," Jeremiah said. He'd started shooting jizz the past winter.

"So? Show us," Gary said. They all started taking their dicks out at the same time, except for PeeVee, who waited to see what they were doing and followed. All of them were hard. Jeremiah examined each and was relieved to see that Gary's was smaller than his. PeeVee's was weird, sort of triangular—thick at the stump and tapered at the head. Peter's was bigger than any of them, and he had the most hair.

"You know how to use it?" Gary said, reaching over and grabbing Jeremiah's boner like it was nothing. Jeremiah couldn't stand it. He closed his eyes. "Look, he's getting off big time," Gary said to Peter. He took his hand away and Peter stepped up to take it. He stroked it even more adeptly than Gary had. Jeremiah had never done anything like this before.

When he opened his eyes again he saw that Gary was stroking PeeVee and PeeVee was stroking Peter.

"Race," PeeVee said flatly.

"That's right, it's a race," Gary said. "Whoever cums first wins. New guy, you stroke mine." Jeremiah looked down. Gary's pert dick was right there. He took it in his hand, stroked it tentatively. It felt kind of cool to feel somebody else's.

PeeVee came first, to Jeremiah's surprise. His breathing got thick, his grunts sounded tortured. He shot a copious load all over the rotted wood of the treehouse.

Peter's hand was unstoppable, and Jeremiah lost it next. His knees buckled as he shot his load, Peter's hand milking every last drop.

Gary and Peter stroked each other off to finish, blowing their loads almost simultaneously. They shook the last drops of cum from one another's dripping dicks.

"Peter lost," Gary announced. Peter got on his knees. "Loser has to clean up." Peter scooted to PeeVee and took his dick in his mouth in one big gulp. He did a clean sweep, from bottom to top, licking it clean. He did the same to Jeremiah, then Gary.

"He always loses," Gary said with a grin.

His grandma asked him where he'd been all afternoon.

"I met some boys down the hill and we were playing," Jeremiah said.

"Playing with the trash," his grandma said.

"No, we weren't playing with trash."

"It's all trash down there," she said. Jeremiah lay in bed that night, wondering if what they'd done was gay. He didn't feel gay. And even if he did, he decided, he'd probably do it again anyway.

The boys were already in the clearing the next morning when Jeremiah got there, and Gary made a big deal of it. He stepped out from behind a bush and blocked Jeremiah's path, his arms folded across his chest.

"What's the secret password?"

"You didn't tell me one," Jeremiah said. Gary seemed exasperated. "Oh, I know: 'I love jerking off,'" he said. They went up to the treehouse where Jeremiah completed even more steps in his initiation. First he had to smoke a cigarette—an old stale Camel Gary pulled out of a crumpled-up pack.

"Next is the most important part. Take down your pants," Gary said. Jeremiah stood up, shrugging. He sort of didn't mind. When he dropped his drawers he already had half a boner. "Close your eyes," Gary instructed. Someone knelt in front of him. Jeremiah knew it was Gary somehow. He felt Gary's mouth enveloping his dick, warm and wet, sliding all the way down and back up. It felt about a million times better than Peter's hand, Jeremiah thought. Gary went down on him again, keeping his mouth tight, his tongue sliding up and down and over it. He kept doing it and Jeremiah suddenly realized he was going to cum. He started to say something but remembered to keep quiet. His sperm came shooting out and still Gary kept sucking him, grunting as Jeremiah's sperm filled his mouth.

Jeremiah had heard of "blowjobs" before but only later did he realize that was what Gary had given him. Gary came off of him and spit over the side of the treehouse.

"Okay, you can open your eyes now," Gary said, smiling and wiping his mouth.

"I can't believe you did that," Jeremiah said.

"Why not? It's fun," Peter said. He was jacking off PeeVee. "Watch," he said, and knelt down before PeeVee, taking all his dick in his mouth.

"Peter loves suckin bone," Gary said. "He'll do it whenever you want." PeeVee kept his hands at his sides as Peter bobbed his head on his dick. His face screwed up in a crude gesture of pleasure and transport, and Jeremiah figured he was coming.

They left a little while later. After he'd eaten lunch, Jeremiah came back.

"Where's PeeVee?" he asked the other two.

"He got in trouble," Peter said.

"What'd he do?"

"He got my cousin's cat and crushed its head in a vice," Peter said.

"Except he didn't even do it," Gary added.

"Who did?" Jeremiah said.

"Guess," Gary said, motioning to Peter, who smiled the

smile of the damned.

Gary pulled a jar of Vaseline out from the knothole. "Peter'll show you a cool way to jerk off," he said. Gary lay on the floor and held his hard dick in the air. Peter got completely naked and straddled Gary's body. He took a glob of Vaseline from the jar and rubbed it into his anus and on to Gary's cock. Jeremiah watched, astonished, as Peter sat down and Gary's dick disappeared into his butt. He rode it, up and down. A smell arose—dank and shitty. Gary's eyes rolled back in his head as Peter bounced on him again and again, his greasy hands making marks where he braced himself on the floor. After a few minutes Gary's stomach muscles tensed up and he closed his eyes. He was cumming right in Peter's butt.

Peter got off him, smiling. "Want to try it?" he asked Jeremiah. Jeremiah shook his head. Gary's cock was limp and covered in slime. Peter sat back and jerked all over himself while Jeremiah watched him, like he was a sideshow. Then Peter got down and squatted in the bushes.

"It's cornholing," Gary said.

"It's gross."

"No it ain't. You just gotta try it."

Jeremiah almost didn't go back the next day, but by early evening boredom had taken its toll. Nobody was there when he arrived. He tried to find the place where Peter had squatted yesterday. He looked at the jar of Vaseline, stuck with dirt and pine needles.

Someone crept up the path and jumped out at him. "Scared ya, didn't I?" Gary said.

"No," Jeremiah said. Gary climbed into the treehouse and grabbed the magazines. He sat next to Jeremiah and flipped through one. "Where's Peter and PeeVee?"

"PeeVee's still in trouble," Gary said. "Peter's at Bob's."

"Who's Bob?"

"He's a guy who lives in the house up the tracks. Peter goes over there all the time."

"He's like an old guy?"

"Yeah, but all the kids go over there. Well, just the boys. He doesn't like girls. He gives you money if you let him take pictures of you and stuff." Jeremiah thought about what Gary said but it didn't make sense. "It's no big deal," Gary said. "I got twenty bucks from him last time I was there."

"Weird."

"He's alright," Gary said. They looked at their magazines in silence. "Got a bone yet?" Gary asked. Jeremiah nodded. Gary reached over to feel. "Let's take em out." They unzipped and pulled down their shorts. Jeremiah felt more excited than he had even the last two days, maybe because he could anticipate what was coming, maybe because it was just him and Gary. They stroked each other's dicks.

"Use the Vaseline, it feels better," Gary said, and smeared some on their dicks. They jacked each other off for a while, slow and steady. Gary was being cool. He'd let go of the bully/leader act and was matching Jeremiah stroke for stroke. Jeremiah realized how he felt close to him. They were on the same wavelength; their emotions were matched.

They got very close to cumming so they stopped.

"I can't believe how good that's feeling," Gary said. "You do it even better than Peter."

"Is Peter gay?" Jeremiah asked.

"Probably," Gary said. "He's alright though."

"I hate him,' Jeremiah said. "What he did yesterday was so gross."

"Cornholing? You just ain't tried it," Gary said. "I like it even better than fucking cunt."

"You've done that?"

"Yeah. We brought Peter's sister down here before and took turns fucking her. But I still thought cornholing was better." They started stroking one another again. "You should try it," Gary said.

"I don't know."

"Try it on me." Jeremiah looked at Gary, who sort of half smiled. He let go of Jeremiah's dick and stood up to take off his

128

pants. "I've done it before." He got on all fours, his ass spread before Jeremiah. Jeremiah looked at his smooth white cheeks, his small pink hole.

"C'mon, just grease up your bone. Put the tip in just to see."

"Won't it hurt?"

"Not too bad. Besides, I don't care." He wiggled his ass at Jeremiah. He got impatient and grabbed the Vaseline, put some on his hole. He handed Jeremiah the jar and Jeremiah greased his dick. "Line it up good and let me go back on it," Gary said. It took a minute of wriggling around to find the right position, but finally they managed to sink it inside. Gary cried out and gnashed his teeth but he wouldn't let Jeremiah take it out. "Okay, you can go deeper," he finally said. Jeremiah continued. It felt wrong and right at the same time. He knew it was dirty, but it was so tight and hot around his dick.

"You can fuck me if you want, now. Slide it out then back in." Jeremiah took a deep breath and did it. He watched his dick come out of Gary's ass. It wasn't covered in brown or anything. What was weird was the idea of being inside someone, of having their insides grip you.

"Fuck me," Gary panted on Jeremiah's third pass. That was all it took. Jeremiah lost it, his thighs quivering as his load shot out. The whole thing had lasted just minutes.

Gary crouched in the bushes afterward just like Peter had. He tossed Jeremiah a piece from the wet pile of clothes to wipe up. Gary used the same shirt afterward to wipe his ass.

Jeremiah took a long shower that night. He could still smell it on his fingers, though, as he lay in bed. Vaseline and Gary's ass.

The next morning he had to go to church with his grandma, but he got away that afternoon. He descended Lear Hill, took the now-familiar path into the woods. The three of them were there, but they didn't notice Jeremiah as he approached.

They were cornholing PeeVee next to the tree. Peter was doing it first, then Gary. They were rough, holding PeeVee's head down, slapping his ass, laughing. Jeremiah tried to figure out if PeeVee was enjoying it or not. From where he stood, though, it was impossible to tell.

14. Adult

Sess Roberts wiped a glob of bluish-white cum off of the black-painted wall and tried to recall the allure a porno-clerk job once held for him. There was more cum on the floor of the stall (or "buddy booth," as they called the enclosures) but he let that go. He had nine more to clean and he was tired.

He could hear obscene wet sloshing coming from dedicated regular Lloyd Donahue's stall as he zipped past. Lloyd had given up approaching Sess after the fourth or fifth week, for which Sess was thankful, but it was better to avoid contact if at all possible, especially since they were the only ones in the store. At least he wouldn't have to clean up Lloyd's load until tomorrow morning; all the better to let his germs dissipate a little.

It wasn't like he'd ever held illusions about the job—he'd known what he was getting into. For nearly a year before he applied for work he'd been adding his own DNA to the wealth of genetic material on the arcade walls, when it wasn't being guzzled down by the minivan-and-wedding-band set, that was.

He dumped the pail of scummy water in the back room sink and stepped outside for a smoke. The dark highway lay before him, stretching out in both directions. Maybe it was silly, but the highway was part of what drew him to the job. It was four a.m., that netherworld between night and morning. Every other minute or so a car would fly by in a red and white streak, leaving a lonely sound in its wake. Who were they? Where were they going? He was just a blip, a speck on a point on a map. But even in the smallest of places there were huge things happening, whole worlds nobody would ever know about.

He snubbed out his cigarette in a coffee can nailed to the side of the building. He heard a motorcycle—a Harley—approaching. It slowed as it neared the building and turned into the parking lot.

Sess ducked inside, behind the counter. The bell rang as the biker walked inside, then turned toward him and smiled. That was unusual. Most patrons slithered behind the shelves and never made eye contact. The biker's grin was big and handsome. If Sess hadn't been so taken off guard he would've smiled back.

"Howdy," the biker said. He was in his forties. He was hot.

"Can I help you?"

"I hope so," he said in a gravelly voice, resting his golden brown arms on the counter. "Do you know how far it is to Cleveland?"

"Cleveland? Jesus—no. I think at least three hours, maybe four?"

"You ever been there?"

"No."

The biker stretched, raising his arms over his head. His leather jacket and black T-shirt rode up, exposing a thick, tan stomach.

"Oh well," he said. He reached into his pocket. "Ten tokens please." Sess poured the tokens into his hand. "Long night for ya?"

"Long enough," Sess answered.

"Tired, huh?"

"A little."

"I'm gonna get some relief myself," the biker said. He winked, then vanished into the dark arcade.

Sess had known about the porno store since he was young; everyone in Groom did. It was on Route 428, right on the edge of town. The sign alone screamed sex; pitch-black letters on a lit-up yellow background that simply said ADULT. Mothers would try to shame ingoing patrons by honking their horns as they drove past, and concerned women had led campaigns over the years to shut it down. Still it stood, a monument to the elephant in everyone's rooms. The women knew what went on in there, or thought they did. The point was that they thought about it.

What Sess hadn't known about was the arcade. He'd found out about that through a website, *cruisingforsex.com*, staring in open-mouthed wonder at the computer screen to see that here, in the tiny nowhere town of Groom, Pennsylvania, there was not one but *two* places listed where people could go for anonymous gay sex.

He'd tried the other place first—Promised Land State Park, which was just up the highway from Wal-Mart. He spent some time hanging around in his mom's Cavalier and later on the playground swings, dragging his feet on the ground. One guy walked past him. He wore a windbreaker and had beady eyes, and as soon as Sess made eye contact he knew. The guy hung around the parking lot, but Sess didn't know what to do so he ignored him. He was relieved when the guy left.

Being underage, he'd had to work up some nerve to try the porno store. He walked there the first time, fearful of someone spotting his mom's Cavalier. It was a good twenty-minute walk from his house, along a backcountry road that ended right at the highway, the porno store about fifteen yards from that. To stay out of view, he crept along the sharply sloping hillside behind the store, twisting his ankle and slashing his arms on thorny branches.

The lot behind the store, shielded from the highway and ringed by the woods, was a world unto itself. Yellow sodium lights had kicked on in the waning evening light, illuminating at least five cars, four with men sitting inside. Their eyes followed Sess as he nervously opened the back door.

The adult store, inside, was both thrillingly alien and disappointingly mundane, mainly white shelves lined with videos and DVDs. The boxes displayed colorful pictures of pink holes and engorged organs. The fluorescent lighting made it look like Rite-Aid, only with dildos.

The overweight guy behind the counter (the owner, he'd later find) looked at him as he entered. Sess braced himself for the worst. But the guy just smiled; an icky smile that let Sess know exactly what he was thinking.

Sess had never considered himself a good-looking kid. He was tall and gangly, with flat, black, boring hair and a jaw that sloped into his neck rather than jutting out. But it didn't take long to sense that here he was the belle of the ball. Had this been a cartoon the clerk would have had a thought bubble of a steaming, freshly cooked chicken hovering over his head. He didn't card Sess, didn't say anything but "Have a good time," and handed him his tokens.

Sess thought about heading into the arcade to cruise the biker. Sex on the job was expected, even encouraged by the owner, who'd addressed it during his interview.

"Just do it in the center booth and keep the door open a little so you can see if anybody's trying to steal shit," he'd said. He took Sess on a tour of the place, principally to corner Sess in that center booth and take out his cock. It was impressive and would've been intriguing had it not been attached to such a repugnant person.

"It's nice," Sess demurred, then pushed past the guy. He may have been naïve but he was not about to blow a big-titted greaseball for a porno-shop job.

Sess heard Lloyd shuffling around in the arcade and hoped the biker had sense enough to turn the old troll away. Truth was, he wasn't sure about the biker. He'd gathered a good deal of experience with cruising in the past year, but something about the biker threw him off. He seemed too confident, too self-contained. Sess wondered if he was straight.

He feared rejection. A few weeks after Sess had started coming to the arcade, he'd gathered up enough courage to approach a hot college guy around his age, a rarity in the place. The guy sat there, looked him up and down, and simply shook

134

his head as though Sess was one of a choice of entrée selections that he didn't care for. The sympathetic look Lloyd gave him on his way back to his booth only made it worse.

So the biker went about his business in the dark and Sess kept behind the counter, watching the goings-on in the back lot via a fuzzy, black-and-white monitor mounted under the counter. The owner didn't care if people cruised out there, but he liked to keep an eye on things. Sess watched a car drive in, poke slowly through the mostly empty lot, and continue on its lonely way.

The porno store became a refuge for Sess during his last year of high school, a safe house for some beleaguered central part of him that most everyone—his asshole Catholic parents especially—wanted to ignore. The store was his burning secret, the sly smile on his face when he walked down the chaotic halls of Groom Senior High. The sexuality that had lain dormant and unacknowledged since junior high was now alive and kicking and powerfully real.

He didn't have any real friends in high school, just acquaintances. He wore black and listened to Nine Inch Nails and cultivated a personality that was above and beyond humanity. He got harassed a lot, even early on. It was like they could sniff it out. By his junior year people were harassing him in class, coughing "fag" under their breath. They practically knew before he did.

The worst was Dan Frye, running back for the Groom Bobcats and Chief Asshole of the school. He'd hone in on Sess in the hallway, approaching him slowly, getting closer so that the minute their sides touched he could slam hard against Sess's shoulder, knocking him off balance and spinning him around.

135

He'd put his lips to Sess's ear and in a throaty snarl he'd say the magic word.

Dan wasn't like the others. He didn't need a crowd or an audience; he wasn't making fun or provoking laughter. That was what made him so dangerous. For him it was personal. It was serious.

Which made it all the sweeter when Sess fucked Dan's dad just prior to graduation.

That day had started out with frustration. His parents were gone for the weekend, and the lilting promise of unquestioned hours away from home had been crushed hard by an unusually desolate Friday night in the arcade. For what felt like hours he fed tokens into the TV, nobody but Lloyd and the usual suspects cruising past his booth, hoping for a bite. Then a new guy passed his booth. For a split second he looked in, caught Sess's eye, and that was all it took.

Sess had noticed Dan Frye's dad before. It was sort of impossible not to. The guy was built like a battleship, exhibiting his body with impunity in tight polo shirts with buttons undone, the smooth hard mounds of his cleavage eclipsing his wife's, his beefy butt encased like sausage meat in his jeans, a healthy crotch packed tight up front. He was a stud, plain and simple, and had the same air of cocky assholery as his son.

Sess crept up to his stall. The sliding door of the older man's booth was open and he stuck his head inside. Tom Frye was sitting on the small bench across from the TV, watching straight porn. He looked at Sess (he didn't seem to recognize him) with a detached gaze and grabbed his crotch as an invitation. Sess stepped inside and slid the door shut. He thought he heard Lloyd's dejected sigh.

Sess knelt on the floor. He unbuckled Tom's pants, revealing stylish black bikini briefs. The older man was completely hard. Sess took it out. Tom drew air in through his nose, his head back and his eyes closed. His cock wasn't all that large, but that wasn't the point. His pubes were trimmed to a neat crew cut; his balls were shaved. Sess wondered if Dan's cock was similar.

He slid it down his throat. Tom didn't make a sound. A pass, another pass and already Tom's legs were tensing up, so Sess backed off. He tapped Tom under his arms and Tom got the message and stood up. Despite the guarded, hostile air Tom gave off in public, he was pliant and accommodating inside the booth, in the moment. He let Sess turn him around and strip the briefs from the firm mounds of his butt. Sess caressed the ass like it was a crystal ball. This was an absolute coup.

He buried his face in Mr. Frye's butt. Tom couldn't suppress an overwhelmed whimper. He leaned his head against the wall, supporting it with his arm and keeping his eyes shut tight. Sess tongued Tom's crack good but the asshole never truly relaxed. It remained tight and tense, even when Sess wormed a finger inside.

He grabbed lube and a condom out of his jeans pocket, took his pants down and got himself ready. Tom said nothing, just kept his ass backed up as Sess mounted him and worked the head of his dick inside, probably being rougher than he should have, but Tom didn't object.

The porn on the monitor lit up their sex in shifting phosphorescent patterns. Sess, a kid who wasn't even a blip on Tom's radar—but who loomed large on the son's—was now inside a shrine to masculinity, defiling him, using him like a whore. He barely noticed when Tom climaxed, the cum spilling out of his untouched dick and pooling on the bench. Sess came soon after, inside the condom, inside Dan Frye's dad. He might as well have been erecting a flag on the surface of the moon.

❖

Graduation passed and his eighteenth birthday came and Sess applied that very day and got the job. The fact that his parents hated it made it that much sweeter. They threatened to kick him out of the house.

"Do it," he said, eating his Frosted Flakes, knowing they would never. He was their only child, the buffer for their anxieties in a loveless marriage, and without him they'd collide and fall apart.

His shift was from eleven p.m. to six a.m., during which time he sampled from a wholly exhaustible succession of cocks, mouths and assholes. Only recently had it grown stale, all the secrecy and shame and cum for cum's sake. When they were done they zipped up and got out, went home to their wives and their beaten-down lives, their throats raw from sucking him off, their hands cramped from milking his precious elixir, for wasn't he the fountain of fucking youth? Couldn't his cum restore them to a life of promise and vitality, a time before children and mortgages and exercise equipment that collected dust in the basement rec room?

His cum was a truth serum for those living a lie.

He wiped it away every shift, wasted potential spackled to the stalls and drooling off the walls. How long did it take for sperm cells to die?

※

The biker spent half an hour in the arcade. When he emerged he looked almost hurt. He walked up to the counter.

"Nice booths you got there," he said.

"They're okay."

"I guess you've seen enough of this place."

"Pretty much, yeah."

The biker looked down at his boots. He raised his head. "I'm Ron," he said, holding out his hand. Sess shook it. It was tough and solid. It had integrity. Sess introduced himself.

"Cleveland, huh?" Sess said.

"Yep. Thought I'd make it there tonight but guess not. Maybe I oughta crash here—is there a motel nearby?"

"Yeah, there's a Best Western about ten miles west."

"Care to join me?" he said.

"I'm working," Sess said, laughing. Ron brightened. He'd cracked Sess's armor.

"When do you get off?"

"Six."

"Hmmm...don't know if I can hold off that long."

"You didn't do anything in the booth?"

"I mean hold off without sleep. But no, I didn't do anything in the booth. I was hoping you'd stop by."

"We could still," Sess said, already walking around the counter. Ron stepped up to him. For a moment Ron let the sizzling space between their bodies be. Then he took the younger man in his arms and kissed him. They broke apart and Ron shot him a widescreen grin. *Funny*, Sess thought, *how you never notice the absence of things.*

They went into the arcade. Lloyd was still in the center stall so they took a back booth. He wouldn't be able to monitor the front, but he was past that. Ron reached down to feel his package and looked at him in surprise. He'd found Sess's secret weapon. They massaged each other through their jeans for a while, making out and staying so, so close.

Ron went down on him. He had technique, taking Sess's cock in slowly, savoring every inch, letting it fill his throat before sliding back up. He kept his eyes on it, massaging Sess's balls, then hungrily going down on it again and Sess felt it in his toes. Ron breathed heavily through his nose as he worked Sess's dick, his tongue thickly slathering the underside.

He heard the bell ding on the door and realized Lloyd had left. Ron stood up and freed his cock. It was fat, stout, perched atop two hearty balls under a nest of dark hair. Sess took it in his hand and dropped to his knees. It was a suckable cock and Sess took full advantage of its party size. Ron was a leaker. Sess liked that. He licked it right off of Ron's cockhead, hot and fresh.

He felt Ron's body, tight and smooth with a smattering of hair across his chest. He tweaked Ron's nipples and the biker moaned. The moans cut through the silence of the store. Normally you didn't make any noise, but it was just them, just now.

Ron turned around and dropped his black jeans over his butt, which was smooth as an egg and nut brown in color.

"You're so tan," Sess said.

"I like to ride naked whenever possible," Ron said. He kicked off his jeans and widened his stance, revealing a buttcrack lined with fine hair that ringed around his pink asshole.

Sess ate him out. Ron's butt was clean but sweaty from a day spent on the road. He tentatively touched a finger to Ron's hot hole, trying to gauge his reaction. Ron reached back, took hold of his hand, and pressed Sess's finger inside of him. It was tight and hot.

"You wanna fuck me?" Ron said.

"Sure," he said. Ron smiled.

"You got a rubber?"

"Definitely." Pants still around his ankles he shuffled into the store, coming back with supplies. Ron laughed.

"I'll need to sit on it first," he said. Sess got on the bench and let Ron lower himself onto his cock. He was facing him as he did it and Sess watched his expression, the hot flash of pain as Sess's cock first pierced inside, then a gradual letting go until he was bouncing up and down on Sess, his hard cock bobbing in time.

"How do you want me?" he asked.

"Huh?"

"How do you wanna fuck me? From behind?"

"Okay."

So he fucked Ron doggy-style. Only then did he realize they were in the same booth in which he'd fucked Dan Frye's dad. The same thing—fucking—but it was completely different. Where Tom had been stiff and scared, Ron was loose and free, backing up to meet his thrusts, reaching back to grab Sess's ass and pull him in deeper.

Sess had yet to bottom with a real dick. And though he'd experimented with whatever phallic-shaped object was lying around the house, he thought that anal sex wasn't something a guy with a dick up his ass enjoyed—it was being dutiful, an act of martyrdom. For Tom Frye it had seemed a chore, a dirty deed. Ron seemed to get fucked right up into a higher plane of existence.

"I'm gonna cum," Ron said, and his hand clenched around Sess's ass cheek. He found Sess's hole with his finger and pressed it tight. Sess cupped his palm in front of Ron's dick and caught his load. He brought it to his tongue and it tasted good. He lapped it up as he power-fucked the biker, swallowing it as Ron's finger pressed into his ass and he started losing it himself. His knees went weak as spurt after spurt of jizz filled the condom in Ron's ass.

Ron kissed him again when they broke apart.

Sess got some paper towels. "Thanks," Ron said, as Sess wiped the lube from his butt.

"Just doing my job." He got dressed and scanned the store. No damage, no foul.

"Let's talk," Ron said as he swaggered out of the arcade, still buckling his belt. "What are you doing these days?"

"What do you mean?"

"I'm headed west. On my bike. There's a place in California, just south of San Francisco. A little beach town, some friends of mine have a community out there." Sess looked at Ron. "There's room on the bike," he said, smiling. "I think you should come with me."

"Right now?"

"If you want. But I need some sleep. Tomorrow, then. Early."

"I have to work tomorrow."

"Not *really*," Ron said. "You don't *have* to do anything except live or die, right?"

"I live with my parents."

"I'll pick you up there."

"I only have a couple hundred bucks."

"That's enough," Ron said. Sess shuffled his feet. "Give me your address," Ron said. "I'll stop outside tomorrow. Nine a.m., so don't sleep late. I'll honk the horn and if you don't come out I'll keep going." Sess wrote his name and address on a receipt. "Sess. I thought you were saying Seth. My last name's Wood; friends call me Woody."

They shook hands. Ron put a hand on his shoulder and looked in his eyes.

"Don't think about it," he said. He leaned forward, gave him another kiss, and took off. The sound of his Harley faded as it cruised down the highway.

Sess looked at his empty store. He knew what he wanted to do in his heart, but that was such bullshit. People said "follow your heart" like it was an easy thing to do. There was a lot of space between your heart and your brain, a lot of bundled up nerves and connections that didn't always carry the message.

He thought about his dog at home, Cougar. The minute Sess walked in the door Cougar would wrap around his legs in ecstatic circles. He'd curl up next to him in bed as he slept, whether it was for a couple of hours or until late afternoon.

He thought about Cougar and he started to cry, right there in the store, because his bags were already packed. He was gone.

15. The Homo Hut (II)

Dom didn't know he was horny, at first. He'd simply decided to take a shower and head home. When he came out of his cabin (it doubled as an office for the gay campground that he and his partner Randy co-owned), Todd caught site of him.

Todd was their part-time employee, a local guy who started camping there so much they'd taken him on as a handyman. He'd been walking up the road with a half-full trash bag in his hand. When he saw Dom standing at the door of his cabin he stopped. Slowly, deliberately, he looked Dom up and down.

"Afternoon, boss," Todd said, his lips curling into a smile.

"Afternoon," Dom said. He turned to lock the door, well aware of Todd's eyes scanning his backside. *No wonder he can't keep his eyes off me*, he thought as he descended the wooden steps to where Todd was standing in the road. *My clothes couldn't be any goddamn tighter.*

That was when he realized it. Dom had spent the morning clearing a felled tree away from campsite number nine—hard work, and he'd felt it in his body as he'd walked back to the cabin. Everything felt tight and toned. So after a long shower he'd reached for a thin, tight T-shirt and clingy basketball shorts. But the kicker was the skimpy briefs he'd worn underneath, which were high-cut and tighter than tight. Like a lot of his briefs, they rode up the crack of his beefy, melon-shaped butt, and the seams must have been obvious to Todd's devouring eyes. He hadn't purposely dressed horny—his unconscious exhibitionist streak had taken over. Even after all this time, thirty years of being out of the closet, having sex with his boyfriend and quite a few other beautiful men, he was still slow on his own uptake.

"How's the litter situation?" Dom said. He walked right up to Todd, letting the younger guy get an eyeful of the bulge in front of his shorts.

"Not bad," Todd said, not trying to hide where his eyes were roaming. "Not too many guys stayed last night anyway."

"Yeah, I know," Dom said.

"I might take a break. Drink a beer down by the lake. Want to join me?" Todd said, casually lifting his shirt to reveal and rub his flat, hairy stomach. Dom considered it. Todd was in his late twenties and had a cute ass that had a reputation for being quite accommodating. The thought of Todd letting him pork his butt down by the river was pretty damned appealing, but Dom knew better than to screw his employees.

"Maybe some other time. I'm headin home. Think you can hold down the fort till I get back this evening?"

"Yeah, no problem," Todd said, hooking his thumbs into the waistband of his jeans to reveal the top of his pubic bush. "Some other time, then."

Dom gave him one last glance as he lowered himself into his car. He smiled to himself. If, at fifty-two years old, he could still make a guy of Todd's age lick his lips, he figured he was doing alright.

As Dom pulled up to his house in Groom, an eighteen year-old football player with a hard-on was in his living room, crying on his partner Randy's shoulder.

"I gotta get the door," Randy said, and pulled the kid away. Dan Frye rubbed the tears from his eyes with a fist, but he couldn't look at Randy, or anything but his own feet, his head weighty with shame, the façade of his cockiness long gone. Randy craned his neck to try to catch the kid's gaze. He looked like an eight year old who'd lost his favorite stuffed animal. "I'll send whoever it is away. Just let me get it real quick or they'll

keep knocking."

Randy took a deep breath as he walked toward the back door. As much as he got exhausted with living in this town, as much as he felt he knew every position of every molecule in every last person, building, and street like the back of his goddamned hand, the town still managed to surprise him.

He got another surprise when he opened the door to find his lover, Dom, standing at the doorway.

"Why's the door locked?" Dom said. "I forgot my key at camp."

"I must've locked it last night when I got back," Randy said.

"Got back from where?" Dom said, stepping inside the house. He sidled up to Randy and pulled him in for a kiss, wrapping his arm around Randy's waist and bringing their bodies tight together. Their lips found each other. Dom slipped his tongue inside Randy's mouth. As they kissed, he took Randy's hand and brought it to his butt. Randy felt his rational mind slipping away. He palmed his lover's firm buttcheek. He started to get hard.

Dom put his lips to Randy's ear. "Please fuck me," he whispered. He stuck his hand between their bodies and found Randy's growing cock. "Do whatever you want with me, man, I just need to get fucked so bad."

Dom considered himself versatile, but he usually only topped with cute young things. In fact he'd started out fantasizing about Todd on his ride home, envisioning the younger guy's cocky little butt spread wide for him as he pinned Todd's hands against a tree, working his cock inside and fucking away until he came in that sweet butt, never mind if Todd got off or not. He saw his own ass rising and falling as he humped Todd, then he imagined Todd reaching back and sticking a finger in his ass as he got closer to blowing...and then his thoughts had turned to Randy.

Nobody had ever been able to fuck him quite like Randy. Maybe it was the trust they'd built up with each other over the years, but even when they'd been young Randy's quiet confidence never failed to turn Dom's knees to jelly.

So hauling down the highway he'd thrown one leg up on the dash, wet his finger in his mouth, slid it up the pant leg of his shorts and fingered himself; imagining Randy taking him from behind, from the front, from wherever Randy damn well pleased.

Randy took his hand away from Dom's butt and pushed at his chest as if to pull apart from him, but Dom grabbed his wrist and forced his lover's hand down the back of his shorts. "Feel me," Dom said. "I'm fucking moist. I'm totally ready." He felt Randy's finger poke inside his smooth and spit-slicked asshole. Randy pushed it in to the first knuckle. "Oh fuuuuck," Dom whispered. "C'mon man, bend me over the goddamn table, I don't care..."

But Randy was regaining his senses. "Uh, just a sec, lover," he said, taking his hand from between Dom's cheeks and pulling apart from him. "We, um, have a visitor."

Dom followed Randy's gaze to the doorway of the kitchen, and saw a high-school-aged boy standing there, watching them, his face a mixture of shock and fascination.

"Jesus, I didn't realize," Dom said, futilely pulling his shirt out in front of him to cover his erection. But what was this? The kid had a frigging circus tent in his cargo shorts.

"This is Dan Frye," Randy said nonchalantly, putting his hand on the boy's shoulder. "You know—Tom Frye's son from down the street?"

"Oh, sure," Dom said, reflexively reaching out to shake the kid's hand. The kid took it. He looked like he'd been crying, and there was an intensity to his glare that made Dom take a step back.

"This is my boyfriend, Dom," Randy said to Dan. Dan nodded his head matter-of-factly. Introductions weren't necessary. He'd always known who they were. For as long as he could remember, he'd known. Of course the idea of them had always instilled in him a deep and abiding hatred, just as it did with his dad. His dad practically raged at the sight or thought of the Spring Street queers, they incited and excited emotions in him like nothing else could. Dan had always taken it as a given that everybody felt this way. And yet, in the last couple of years, he'd begun to realize that this wasn't so.

Every Halloween in Groom kids went "corning," meaning they would raid the cornfield on Derry Lane, gathering the hard kernels into socks and stalking out at night to throw handfuls of it at houses.

"Make sure you get the fags on Spring Street good," Dan's dad had said to him every year since he'd started doing it with his friends.

So this year they'd been shucking the corn in Derrick's laundry room when Dan had come up with a plan to do more to the fags then just throw corn at them. "We'll wrap their house in Saran Wrap," he said. "All the way around so they won't be able to open their doors. Then we'll get shaving cream and write shit on their lawns, just totally go crazy on the place." But his friends—Derrick, Craig, Toby—didn't really care. Worse, they looked at him like *he* had a problem. Were they fags themselves? The thought had crossed his mind.

Now it was summer and he was leaving for college in a couple of months. The notion had begun to take hold they they might never be coming back to Groom. Laying in bed one night after filling out his college application, he realized his whole life could potentially change. None of his friends were going to the college he was planning on attending. He could become whoever he wanted. A hot bolt of excitement and fear shot through his core.

He'd been bored last night, bored and vaguely angry. His dad had a can of spray paint in the garage and he'd decided to use it. Maybe he'd considered getting caught, maybe he hadn't. The circumstances seemed unbelievable, but here he was, standing in their kitchen, and in some way he'd expected to find himself here, eventually.

Randy went to the counter and poured himself a cup of coffee, as much to distract himself from the awkward situation as anything.

"So," he said, turning to Dom. "Is Todd looking after the camp?"

"Uh, yeah..." Dom said. He took his eyes away from the erection in Dan's shorts. "Yeah. Until later tonight."

"Good," Randy said, handing him a mug of coffee. He turned to Dan. "Want some?" Dan nodded, and Randy grabbed a mug from the shelf and poured him some. "Get that tree cleared away?" he said to Dom.

"Sure did," Dom said, watching as Randy handed Dan the mug. "So, uh, what are you guys up to?"

"Well, Dan came by to do some work on the front porch." Randy caught Dom's confused look. "It's a long story, we'll explain it to you later."

"Okay," Dom said. They stood in the kitchen in an awkward silence, sipping their coffees as three boners slowly deflated.

"So Dan, you want to stay for lunch?" Randy offered.

"Sure," Dan said, shrugging.

"Leftovers okay?" Dom and Dan nodded. "Alright then," Randy said. "Dom, I'll help you grab your stuff out of the car."

"My stuff?" Dom said dumbly. Randy widened his eyes at him. "Oh yeah, thanks."

"Just make yourself at home," Randy said to Dan; then he herded Dom out the back door. They stood next to Dom's truck and Randy breathlessly explained all that had happened— the late-night wake-up call, Tom Frye in his undies, Dan's reappearance that morning, Dan's boner and subsequent crying on his shoulder.

"Wow," was all Dom could say, as much impressed and jealous by Randy getting a glimpse of Tom Frye in his underwear than by any other portion of the story. Then he cautiously added: "Do you think he wants to like, do something with us?"

"Oh, geez. I don't know. I don't think we should, do you?"

"He's kinda hot."

"Jesus Christ, Dom. He's confused as hell is what he is. But I'm afraid he'll be more upset if we make him go home. So let's just talk to him and see where it goes."

"Okay. Let me get my composure for a second before I go back in there, okay?"

"No problem babe," Randy said, and gave his lover a kiss on the cheek. Randy went around the outside of the house and in through the front porch.

"You did a good job covering it up," he said to Dan once he got inside.

"What?" Dan said, looking defensive.

"The front porch. The graffiti. You painted over it well."

"Oh," Dan said, softening. "Yeah. Thanks. I...I'm really sorry," he said.

"It's okay,' Randy said. He took the kid by the shoulder. "You know, I don't think you're a bad kid. Really, I don't. And if you ever want to come by, for any reason at all, you're always welcome here." Tears started to well up Dan's eyes again. "You don't have to stay right now if you don't want to."

"I want to stay," Dan said. He looked at the floor. "I...I want to see what you guys were doing. Earlier."

"Oh," Randy said. "You mean like when I was kissing Dom?"

"Yeah," Dan said. Randy observed a lurch in the front of the kid's shorts. He took his hand away from the kid's shoulder.

"It's been a long day," Randy said. "Why don't you, you know, rest on it and come back some other time?"

"No," Dan said flatly, feeling acutely that this was *the time*, maybe the only time he'd have the courage to do something about...about what? His curiosity. That was what it was, wasn't it? "I want to stay."

Dom came inside. He sidled up to Randy and wrapped his arm around his back. He put his other arm around Dan's tight

150

waist. Dan didn't pull away. Dom reached down and felt the kid's hard cock. Dan shuddered like a motor in the winter. He shook with each breath, but that slowed as he relaxed into Dom, who was massaging his cock through his shorts. He was warmed up them, firing on all cylinders, and he turned to face Dom, who nuzzled the kid's neck.

Randy came behind Dan. He pressed his body to the kid's backside, sandwiching him between him and Dominic. Dan relaxed against him. Randy took a deep breath. He reminded himself that he'd given the kid a choice, that this was what Dan had wanted. Of course he'd known that from the instant they'd laid eyes on each other. But Christ, Dan could turn on them both before it was all over. Run home to his dad, say he'd been assaulted. In an instant the whole town could turn against them.

Risks and rewards. Randy ran his hands up the kid's shirt, feeling his hard, smooth teenage muscles. Dan moaned. He stretched his torso upward to meet Randy's caress. Dan's body was perfect, fatless, his stomach which was crunched up into six tight little nuggets, his pelvis flat and smooth like a cutting board, little slots on either side that shot into the darkness of his shorts.

Dom unbuckled the kid's belt. His shorts fell to the floor. The kid's thick and perfect cock gouged right out of the open fly of his boxer shorts. Randy slid off Dan's boxer shorts and helped him to step out of them. Dan's cock had a pearl of precum on the tip, and the rest of his cockhead was slicked with it. It ran down his shaft in a stream, right to his hairless, hanging balls.

Dom took the kid's cock in his hand. Dan's hips moved with Dom's strokes, smooth and fluid. Dom knelt down and took a deep whiff the kid's fresh body.

Risks and rewards. Once Randy had thought he'd lost his sister to a risk; had questioned whether the rewards had been worth it. But she'd forgiven him eventually, somehow. In retrospect to call what he'd done a risk, or even a decision, seemed almost laughable. Life careened ahead while you struggled to hang on. He hadn't gotten in its path then and he

151

wasn't going to now.

Randy lifted the kid's shirt off of his head. Dan stood naked before them, his head lifted to the ceiling as Randy and Dom explored this as-yet-discovered country. Dom tasted the head of Dan's cock. The kid squinched his eyes, shut them tight. Dom went down on him, all the way to his balls. Dan's face was clenched, pained.

"Open your eyes," Randy whispered into the kid's ears. Dan fluttered them open for a second but kept them pointed at the ceiling. Dom went down on Dan again and his eyes shut right back up.

"Look at me," Randy said, coming around the face the kid. Dan's chest was heaving. He managed to look at Randy.

"Open your eyes," Randy had to keep reminding the kid. "Keep them open."

Natty Soltesz's stories have been published in anthologies including *Best Gay Erotica 2011* and in the magazines *Freshmen*, *Mandate*, and *Handjobs*. He co-wrote the 2009 porn film "Dad Takes a Fishing Trip" with director Joe Gage. Since 2000 he's published stories on his website, nattysoltesz.com, and he is a faithful contributor to the Nifty Erotic Stories Archive.

Michael Kirwan was born in NYC late 1953. Kirwan began drawing around age 4-5 to create an imaginarily tolerable universal to escape the "reality" of his home life. Raised Catholic (but insultingly not molested), he survived his youthful adventures and soon found himself working at the St. Marks Bathhouse in the Village. He had his drawings published first in Sᴛʀᴏᴋᴇ magazine 1985. Through the years, he has produced hundreds of illustrations and comics for "adult" magazines and displayed his work around the world, but he resides in Los Angeles. He earns a meager living selling original artwork to enlightened collectors and producing commission artwork for those who'd like their personal fantasies captured on paper. Bruno Gmunder Verlag released a collection of Kirwan's illustrations, *Just So Horny*, in 2011. See the full spectrum of his Homofesto in the perverted drawings at KirwanArts.com.